THE CANNIBAL KING

RAVENOUS SPIRITS SERIES
BOOK 3

RON RIPLEY

EDITED BY ANNE LAO
AND DAWN KLEMISH

ISBN: 979-8-89476-317-0
Copyright © 2025 by ScareStreet.com

ENTER THE REALM OF TERROR...

We'd like to take a moment to thank you for your support and invite you to join our VIP newsletter.

Dive deeper into the darkness with exclusive offers, early access to new releases, and bone-chilling deals when you sign up at www.ScareStreet.com.

Let the nightmares begin…

See you in the shadows,
Scare Street

PROLOGUE

The island looked as gray and dismal as ever. Even in the height of summer, with green grass and bushes growing up the cliff walls, and trees visible on the surface, there was always something gloomy about it in Mo's opinion. Now, with winter encroaching and a cold bite in the air, the island looked like a place no one had any business going to. He couldn't understand how or why a community lived in a place so remote and inhospitable. It wasn't his cup of tea.

The way into the dock on the island's western side was not an easy voyage. Many rocks sat like jagged teeth jutting from the ocean. He could only imagine what larger vessels must have endured in the past. Hazards were hidden all around the island, and he had heard that there were many shipwrecks in the area.

Mo's skiff was a small but sturdy vessel that could manage the journey with little difficulty. He didn't carry a deep enough draft to hit most of the rocks, and he could easily steer around any he saw coming.

It had been three days since he dropped the two men off on the island. He hoped he would hear from them before he needed to go out, some message that they had found what they needed and were heading back on their own with the boats from the island. But no such luck. The men had been radio-silent for seventy-two hours.

As much as Mo didn't want to head back to the island, he was a man of his word. He told them he would be there, and so, he was fulfilling his promise. He just hoped that they could hold up their end and meet him once he got to shore.

He wouldn't admit it to anyone, but something about the island didn't sit right with him. It was a creepy feeling, but that wasn't the sort of thing you discussed openly with other adults. It sounded silly, but it's still what he felt. It was like walking down a dark alley at night or investigating a strange noise in the basement. Your rational mind could tell you that there's nothing to worry about, but another part tells you to run the other way.

Three boats were tied up on the small, wooden dock near the end of the inlet that led to the island. The same boats were there before when Mo dropped the two men off. At the time, he had been hopeful that they could hitch a ride back on their own. And maybe they had, and they'd just neglected to tell him. If that was the case, he would be properly annoyed. But until he knew otherwise, he was where he promised to be to pick them up and take them home.

The air around the island seemed a little colder. There was no snowfall yet, but it was crisper. Mo got out, tied his boat to the end of the dock, and then walked the length of the wooden slats to where they met the island and its weed-filled crags.

Shane and Frank were supposed to meet him on the dock. Mo was about ten minutes early, so there was a chance they were still held up with something. Maybe they were with the people of the village, so Mo sat on a rock and waited.

Ten minutes passed, and Mo grew impatient. He waited another ten minutes before he decided to have a look for himself. Annoyed as he was, he wouldn't feel right leaving if he didn't make sure they weren't around. Neither man had seemed flighty. They seemed like decent, reliable guys, so he was willing to give them the benefit of the doubt. He would, however, give them grief for making him climb up the side of a cliff to get to the top of the island and look around. Going for a hike had not been part of the deal.

Mo made his way up the zigzagging path carved into the cliff that led to the island and stopped to look around. He had never seen the island from that vantage point. The trail led him to a grassy field. To his left was a forest, but a narrow footpath continued to the right, toward the southern end of the island. He saw no signs of people or civilization.

Mo knew there was a village on the island because he often saw people come to town. The footpath had to lead the way, but it appeared to be a long walk. Another frustration.

Grumbling slightly, Mo set down the path on what he hoped was a short, simple journey to wherever Shane and Frank were. A breeze came in from the eastern side of the island, carrying the smell of salt and maybe a hint of rain. He didn't want to be on the island when bad weather came in, and he quickened his pace as a result.

It was a shorter trip than he had expected before he saw the little village. It had been built into a depression, almost a crater, that set it away from everything else. Mo wondered why anyone would build there, but it was not his place to question how other people lived.

There were a handful of cabins; some stone and some wood. He saw no signs of life, though, and when he looked closer, it was clear no one had been in the village for years. The cabins were empty of all but a few pieces of trash.

"Well, where the hell is everyone?" he asked aloud.

There were no footprints in the mud around the cabins. The only conclusion he could draw was that there must have been another village on the island, but he had no idea where to look and had no intention of exploring further.

Mo retraced his steps to the boat and got on board, pondering what to do next. He didn't want to leave anyone stranded, but they had given him little choice.

He took the receiver from his radio and turned the channel.

"Hey Vedder, you got your ears on? Over."

"Go ahead, Mo. Over," came the response, crackling and hollow sounding. He had told his friend Vedder back in the harbor where he was going, a safety precaution he adopted any time he went out.

"I'm at Maple Grove, and no one is here. Not just the guys I dropped off, but everyone. There's a village, but no one's been here in years. You got any idea where the people are in this place? Over."

Vedder's laughter answered him.

"Man, I do not go to hippie island. No idea what they do there. They're probably all frolicking in a field somewhere. Over."

Mo sighed and looked back the way he had come.

"I don't know what's going on here. These boys seemed like good guys, you know? Worried something went down out here. Over."

"I don't know what to tell you, but the forecast is grim. I wouldn't stay out too long if I were you. Over," Vedder replied.

"Yeah, the water is already getting some chop. The rocks out here aren't friendly. I think I'm going to head back. They have boats and radios; they know to hit channel sixteen if they need help. I'll see you shortly. Out."

He hung up the handset and stepped back off the boat, removing the mooring lines in preparation to leave. When he turned the key in the ignition, the boat remained silent. He tried it again, and still nothing.

"God, what now?" He headed down to the bilge to check on the engine. It wasn't the newest boat, but it had been reliable for years, and he rarely had engine trouble.

Mo was barely below deck when he saw that someone had gutted the engine. Hoses and cables were not just removed but torn to pieces. The shaft was yanked out and bent, and fragments of metal, wood, and plastic were strewn about the bilge.

Anger flared in Mo's chest, but he said nothing. He raced back to the cabin and retrieved the radio handset.

"Mayday, mayday, mayday, this is the Red Sturgeon docked at Maple Grove Island. My vessel has been disabled and—" He looked at the radio handset. The cable was no longer connected to the radio. It had been cut.

4

Mo turned around, looking out at the dock and the other boats. He had turned his back for seconds. Seconds! How had someone gotten on deck without him noticing?

The radio crackled, and static filled the cabin, overwhelming the sound of the sea.

"It's time..." a husky voice whispered. Mo stared in confusion and switched the radio off. It crackled again anyway.

"...to die," the voice finished.

Mo backed away from the radio, and the boat lurched under his feet as though a massive wave had hit the side, even though the water was calm. He heard wood splinter, and water began flowing in below deck. Something had broken through the hull.

Mo saw a shape in the dark, a figure in the rushing water, and backed away. The figure was bigger than anything on his boat should have been. He turned quickly, jumping back onto the dock and watching as his boat lurched to one side, taking on water swiftly until she listed to the side and collapsed.

More shapes moved in the water as Mo watched his boat sink. He thought they were fish at first, or maybe sharks from the size of them. But no fins broke the surface, only shadows moving about in the churning, frigid water.

He looked over the edge at the figures swimming along at his side next to the dock and realized they were not fish but men. Not even men. They looked dead. They were bloated bodies with pale flesh pulling away from their skeletons. Some didn't even have eyes; others had been chewed on by sea life, with pieces of their bodies and faces missing, exposing muscle and bone beneath.

Mo stumbled backing away. A scream was trapped in his throat, and he thought his heart might beat out of his chest. He'd never seen anything so horrifying. He had seen dead men in the past, but never anything like this.

Some of the bodies crawled up the hull of his sinking boat. They tore away pieces, punched their fists through the wood, and reduced it to debris in moments. Others crawled over the decks of the boats still tied to the dock. There were dozens of them, all coming toward Mo.

He turned to face the island and ran. The wood clicked loudly underfoot as he quickly crossed the dock and headed for dry land. A terrible wind blew down from above, storm clouds as black as night rolled in, and snow began to fall. There was no gentle transition or buildup. It was as though hell itself had suddenly opened and decided to freeze the world.

Snow battered against Mo, carrying on brutal winds. He pushed onward, desperate to escape the things in the water. He didn't understand where the storm came from, or how it built so quickly and powerfully. Nothing made sense anymore, and all he knew was that he needed to get away.

A man appeared on the path before him, seemingly from nowhere. He was impossibly tall, and lithe like an athlete. His features were obscured in shadows, but nothing could hide the mane of shaggy hair atop his head and the two, great, high-reaching antlers that rose from his skull toward the sky.

Mo jerked to a halt in front of him, still too close to the sea for comfort. Something was covering the man's face.

"Please—"

The man's hand was on Mo's throat, and he plucked him from the ground with ease. Mo kicked and choked, prying an ice-cold hand away from his neck. A single eye stared at him, hidden away in the darkness, and then something tore into his chest. The man had stabbed him.

A blade that was so cold it burned into Mo's breastbone and cracked ribs. Down it pulled, slicing and crunching, gutting him as it reached his stomach and continued deeper. The things from the water scrambled up on shore, and the last thing Mo saw was their wet, slimy hands pulling apart his insides and pushing them into their mouths.

Chapter 1
Search Party

The storm continued to rage outside. Snow battered the village with no end in sight. Shane and Frank had stayed in the Great Hall, as had about half of the villagers. The rest had decided they were safe to return to their homes. After the ghosts that had taken victims from the village into the woods were destroyed, the villagers felt safe to be alone for a little while.

Shane felt they were less safe than ever, but he didn't want to scare anyone. If the Cannibal King came to town, he doubted it would make a difference if they were in the Great Hall or their cabins. If anything, they might be better off spread out.

Hugh Carson, the ghost of a fur trader who had been partially eaten and murdered by the King, was out in the storm looking for the spirit. He knew more about the ghost than anyone else. Shane had only seen the ghost in the shadows. If there was an inside track on him, Hugh would find it. Shane didn't fully trust him, but he was the only resource they had.

What Shane had seen was enough to give him pause. The ghost was a giant, close to seven feet tall, and he had the antlers of a stag attached to his head. He had kept his distance from Shane, however, while Shane dealt with a half-dozen other cannibal spirits. Like Hugh, they were victims of the King, and they had preyed on the people of Maple Grove.

Shane and Frank had only come to the island to find the son of an old army buddy. What they discovered was that the boy had been sacrificed to the island by their de facto leader, a woman named Mallory. She was under the impression that the island was a living thing and that, by sacrificing people, the island was taking care of the rest of them.

In reality, the ghosts that took people were mindless, barely more than animals. They continued their acts of cannibalism even in death, even though they could not truly eat their victims and gained no nourishment from their flesh. They were just repeating the cycle of pain and misery they had experienced in life. The island provided nothing for the ones left over.

Too late, Shane discovered that the ghosts kept the Cannibal King in check. When Shane arrived and began destroying them, he allowed the King to get free. Essentially, he had traded one problem for another, and they were no further ahead than they had been when they arrived. If anything, they were further behind. When they arrived, they had a boat. Now they had no boat and no way to contact anyone off the island.

Mallory had three boats at her disposal when Shane and Frank showed up. Fearful that police would come to the island if Shane returned to the mainland, she had her right-hand man, Blaine, hide the boats somewhere. Mallory and Blaine were dead now, and no one knew where the boats were. One of the residents had a guess, but no one had confirmed it.

With no cell phone signal or radios on the island, there was no way for anyone to get off. They were miles from shore, caught between the United States and Canada, on an inhospitable rock where numerous boats had wrecked in the past. It was very unlikely anyone would come looking for them. Not before the King made a move.

He had no interest in running from a fight. Hugh had told him that the King was more powerful than he was and that there was no way he could fight the ghost. While Shane appreciated that Hugh had more experience, Shane was still eager to put an end to the cycle of death on Maple Grove Island.

The problem was, as Frank had made Shane realize, he wasn't just fighting for himself. Several dozen innocent people were on the island. The ghost would make victims of them all, so the smart move was to get everyone out. Shane could return to take on the King, but the people who couldn't defend themselves needed to get away. They needed the boats.

Shane didn't intend to be insensitive to anyone's plight, but Frank's influence was changing his perspective. Working with Frank took some adjustment, but he was a good man, and Shane was willing to work in a way that met his goals.

"This storm is not letting up," Frank pointed out. It was not the first time it had been observed in the Hall. It was all anyone could talk about.

"No. We're going to have to go for the boats anyway," Shane said.

Heading out in a blizzard was asking for trouble. The cliffs around the island were treacherous, and he assumed the boats were not hidden in an easily accessible place. The blowing snow, ice, and wind made for a dangerous trip. The only upside Shane could think of was that the southern end of the island was much closer to sea level than the northern end. The descent to whatever cove the boats were hidden in, if they were there, would not be that bad. Not as bad as the western dock.

Even though Mallory had believed the island was alive, and that the ghosts were the spirit of the island, Shane had come around to the idea that she was not as crazy as she sounded. Not that he thought the island was a conscious force, and those cannibals were not manifestations of its spirit. But the island seemed to be working with the King to make things harder for the living.

Shane had seen the same thing in the past. Not an island, but a house. His house. Being haunted for so long could affect a place. It didn't make it a living thing, but it didn't leave it stationary and inorganic. The island didn't have thoughts or desires, but it could make things happen. Shane was positive the weather was a manifestation brought on by the island, working with the King. Maple Grove was simply too haunted for its own good.

If Shane's theory was true and the island was causing most of the trouble, waiting would do no one any good. The island could wait forever; the people on it could not. Their best hope was to head out as soon as possible and find a way back to shore.

"Is everyone on board with leaving?" Shane asked Alina.

The young woman had been friends with Jackson. He was in love with her, and it seemed the feelings were not entirely reciprocated, but she was what brought the man to the island in the first place. He wanted to reconnect with her, having lost touch after college. For his trouble, Mallory fed him to a ghost rather than let him leave.

"Yes," she said.

It had not been easy to get the residents of Maple Grove on board evacuating the island. Even when they knew that some of them were being killed by a ghost, they had taken it as a sacrifice that needed to be made. In their minds, the island was taking care of them and providing safety, friendship, and the bounty of maple trees or some other nonsense. Shane could have slapped every one of them in the face.

Most of the people of Maple Grove had escaped a bad life back on the mainland. Some were running from criminal records, some had been abused, and some had debts, were sick, or just didn't fit in. Everyone had a reason to want to stay there, and if that meant putting up with someone else dying, they were willing to do it. But now, faced with the prospect that everyone would die, they had rethought their positions.

It was not a smooth transition. They had tried to kill Shane and Frank more than once. They had burned down a cabin with the two men inside, and they had tried to gun them down in the village and in the woods. Shane had long ago lost interest in helping the people, but Frank was more dedicated to the cause.

It was only after the cannibals began to take people from the village in large numbers, and they got to see Hugh Carson firsthand, that the people realized Mallory had lied to them and they were all in danger.

"We should head out now while we still have some light," Shane said.

Frank nodded and turned to Clint, the man they'd met when they arrived in Maple Grove. Although he had pulled a gun on them on their first meeting, he had been an asset in negotiating with the town and its people. He was childlike in many ways, but he was helpful, and he was as eager to get away from the place as anyone.

"You said you piloted the boats?" Frank asked.

"Two of them," Clint nodded. "I know how they work. I can get them going, I swear."

"I believe you," Shane said. "You can come with us. Brandon, you should come, too."

The younger man sat at one of the Hall's long tables nearby. He looked surprised when Shane called him out.

"Me?" he asked.

"You think you know where the boats are, right?"

"Yeah. I think. Maybe I could just tell you." The fear was palpable in his voice.

Like everyone else in the Great Hall, Brandon had seen the ghosts kill some of the village residents. He had almost been taken when they attacked in one final push before Shane, Frank, and Hugh took them all out. No one wanted to go out and encounter them again, even though Shane had assured them that those ghosts were gone. The King was another matter.

"You said it's hard to find," Shane said.

Brandon made an awkward face, and Clint put a hand on his shoulder.

"We'll find them sooner with your help. Then we can all go," he pointed out.

"Yeah." Brandon was not enthusiastic. "I guess."

The four men got ready to leave, putting on gloves, hats, and scarves to brave the weather. Clint and Brandon bid farewell to friends from the village. They acted like they were going off to war, or to their deaths. Shane couldn't guarantee they weren't, but he was still more optimistic than they were.

It was a stark turnaround to see the attitudes of the villagers in such a short period. Just a couple days earlier, they had been more than happy to sacrifice people to their island, or sit back and let it happen. Shane supposed it was a good thing that they had learned to fear what they were dealing with rather than thinking it was something to be admired or revered. Fear kept people alive. Blind faith did not.

The wind was blowing harsh and cold, blasting them with snow that was very nearly horizontal as it came at them. Shane had expected no less: The weather had a way of adapting itself on the island to be the greatest hindrance possible.

Any signs of their earlier fight with the ghosts were long gone. There was no sign that anyone had even been outside that day. They headed southeast, cutting between buildings until they were out of the small village and wading through knee-deep snow to get to the shallow side of the depression that led up and out of the village.

Clint led the way with Frank right behind. Shane stayed in the back with Brandon, making sure nothing was following them, and keeping an eye toward not just the village but the forest that he knew waited beyond, now obscured by the weather. The Cannibal King was in there somewhere. Hugh had said the north was his home, but he would not remain there for long.

The others were waiting for Shane when he crested the rise from the village. The world was white and blurry to the southeast. The ocean was hidden, and the stony cliffs that surrounded Maple Grove were nowhere to be seen. What awaited was a mystery.

"Lead the way," Shane said to Brandon. He would not let wind and snow keep him there any longer.

CHAPTER 2

THE COVE

Brandon did not move with speed. Shane had to join him, almost dragging him along at some points, until they had gone through the empty fields of snow that led to the southeast edge of the island.

When they got close enough, they heard the ocean crashing against the rocks below. The southern end of the island was the lowest, and the distance from where they were to the sea was not great. Shane guessed that if someone were to jump in a pinch, they would probably survive. Rocks below notwithstanding, anyway.

It was still hard to see the ocean with the blowing snow, but when they reached the edge and looked over the side, Shane made out powerful white caps and the crashing waves hitting the cliffs of Maple Grove.

There was no sign of a cove, but Brandon assured them it was there, they just had to find the spot that led down. It was a path down the cliffside, he said, and very hard to notice. He also explained that he had found it in the summer, so the snow made it harder to see.

According to Brandon, the cove was all but invisible from the island. It was in a recess below the rock, and the island overhung it. But, he said, if you found the path and went down, it was only a short distance around the cliff face before you saw it clearly.

"Does anything look familiar?" Shane asked as they walked the cliff's edge.

"No. Yes. Everything," Brandon answered glumly.

"But you're sure it was here somewhere," Frank said.

"Somewhere. I think," the man replied.

He looked around as though he were locating his parked car. He walked several paces along the cliff, looked back the way he had come, and then walked several more paces.

Shane and Frank had found a cave on the northeast side of the island, so they had some understanding of what they were looking for. The path down to that cave had been fairly well hidden. The way the rocks jutted out from the edge of the island made it easy for such places to be hidden.

"This looks more familiar." Brandon continued eastward along the rocky wall. The waves below were ceaseless, providing a deafening white noise that made it hard to understand what anyone was saying unless they were practically yelling.

Brandon picked up the pace, excited by recognizing a landmark Shane could not see, and was soon half-obscured by the blowing snow.

"You guys!" came a shout from the man ahead of them, half-stolen by the wind. Shane saw him, mostly a silhouette in the snow, waving his arm. Until he couldn't.

Snow swirled, the wind's direction changed to come from the north, and suddenly, the man was gone.

"Brandon?" Frank shouted.

Shane ran awkwardly, forcing his legs harder than normal to get through the snow and follow the vague path Brandon had left. His trail ended at the rock wall. There was a divot in the snow, the shape of a human body like he had fallen over. But not off the cliff; he had fallen forward. Then he was dragged.

"Brandon!"

Shane was on his knees, looking over the edge of the island. He was in the smoothed-out patch of snow where Brandon had been only moments before. The pattern was unmistakable. He had been dragged over the edge.

Clint and Frank joined Shane. Neither man had seen where Brandon had gone. They hadn't noticed anything come for him, but to Shane's mind it was clear enough. There was no way he had fallen over the edge, not with the marks left in the snow.

He did not think the King would show up and sneakily drag someone to their doom. That was not the way such a ghost operated. Which meant there were still other spirits on the island.

Shane had encountered many ghosts in the north that seemed to have almost no willpower and barely put up a fight against him. But against someone like Brandon, who could neither see them coming nor fight against them, they would have been very dangerous.

"Brandon! Brandon, where are you?" Clint held his hands to his mouth to be heard over the wind and the sea.

"You see anything?" Frank looked over the edge.

Shane stared at the water below. For just a moment, he thought he saw something caught in the waves that was dashed against the base of the cliff. It could have been a man in a winter coat, the same dark gray as Brandon's. Or it could have been a trick of the light, the way the snow was blowing, and the rocks. It had only been for a moment, and it did not return. Nevertheless, the feeling in his gut told him that they would not find Brandon.

"No." Shane was not willing to commit to something if it was just speculation.

"These are drag marks," Frank pointed out. "Maybe we ought to get Clint back to the village."

"Maybe." Shane nodded as he got back to his feet.

He scanned the edge of the cliff in both directions, looking out for anything that might sneak over the top to grab him or Frank. There was nothing. Whatever had taken Brandon had chosen its opportunity because he was alone. Like wolves taking the weakest member of a herd, they had snagged Brandon because they could. Because he was available.

"Take Clint. I'm going to look around a little more. If they took Brandon, it means we're close."

Clint stood near both of the men, afraid to wander too far at this point, and shook his head.

"No, we need to stay out here," he said. "We need to find Brandon."

"I'm going to look for him," Shane said, "but it's too dangerous out here. Whatever happened to him could happen to you. It's best if I handle this."

"What if something happens to you, and no one is here to help?" Clint asked.

"I'm not trapped out here with any of these ghosts. They're the ones who are stuck with me," Shane replied.

Clint looked unconvinced.

"I saw the movie where you got that quote from. That guy wound up dead."

"Everyone winds up dead in the end," Shane said, "but I'm not dying on this stupid island. I'll be fine. You guys go."

"You think so?" Frank asked.

Shane nodded, taking another look around.

"Haven't seen a single ghost on this side of the island except for the cannibals. The ones in the north were rooted, almost. Like I had stumbled into their grave. Maybe we found something here."

"Maybe they've just been following us," Frank countered.

"Maybe. But we just got here. Not giving it up now. Take him back, and I'll come get you when I find something."

Frank looked ready to protest but then thought better of it. Shane gave him a nod and clapped him on the shoulder.

"I'll be fine," he said.

"I bet," Frank replied. "Just be careful, and if you find something, let me know before you run in with guns blazing."

"I'll be as cautious as I need to be," Shane replied.

"Not the answer I was looking for," Frank said. Nevertheless, he took Clint and turned away from the ocean, heading back toward the village.

Shane peered over the edge of the cliff again, leaning as far as he dared in the blowing snow, and looked left and right. Nothing looked different. The snow-encrusted gray-black rock could have hidden caves, coves, pathways, anything.

He continued onward in the same direction that Brandon had gone. It seemed like there was nothing behind them, so it was the logical choice to move forward. He traveled for several yards, looking as carefully as he could, and finding nothing. The minutes passed, and the snow fell, filling in his tracks.

Maybe whatever happened to Brandon was a random accident. None of them had seen it. He hadn't made a sound. Maybe he just lost his footing, fell forward, and skidded back in the snow. It didn't have to be a ghost. But Shane's gut told him they were close to what they were looking for, or something they weren't supposed to see. The island did not want them to leave; he knew that much.

He walked another ten yards and then stopped, scanning over the edge. It seemed like more of the same as the snow swirled around and the waves crashed. Everything was monotone and boring. The world had become a smudge, just the way the island wanted it to be. Forgettable and impossible to track.

Shane was just turning away when he caught a pair of eyes staring up into his from the crags in the wall below. A face, huddled, looking through cracks in the stone.

It was deadly thin, with sunken cheeks and cracked lips. The skin had turned a disgusting, maggoty white. The eyes in the head of the spirit were sunk in deep and almost as milky as the flesh. But they stared into Shane's and then, when it realized he could see it, the ghost scuttled away, heading down a path that Shane wouldn't have believed was there if he hadn't seen the ghost crawling across it.

The cliff face created an illusion that hid the dimensions and made the path look like flat rock. Shane had to lean out as far as he dared and turn his head back to see that it extended out from the side of the wall by several feet.

It took practically standing right at the path's start to even realize where it was, and by then, the ghost he had seen was long gone. But it had followed the path down and around a curve, halfway between the island's surface and the ocean. It had to be what Brandon had told them about. It had to be the way to the mysterious cove he had seen.

Snow covered the path, obscuring it further, and the angle made it a treacherous walk. Shane kept one hand on the side of the cliff as he descended, bracing himself as best he could as he was buffeted by the wind.

If the island sought to destroy him, it relented long enough to let him find his footing. The wind became no fiercer and the snow no more blinding. Shane descended at an almost too-steep-to-handle angle until he reached a flat plateau, the same path that he had seen the ghost on moments earlier.

The spirit had left no footprints, but Shane followed the route it had taken and found it curved around a stony outcropping and into a crevice. As he took the corner, he saw below what Brandon had told them about. There was an opening, invisible from above, like a small lagoon connected to the ocean. A small half-circle of stone protected it from the open sea like a closed-off pool with a small entryway to the south. The water was far less choppy, and there was even a small beach, though it was snow-covered and dismal.

Shane sighed audibly as he looked down. It would have been a good place to hide the boats had someone thought of it, but nothing was there. The boats were still missing. The only thing he could think was that they had been destroyed—by the ghost, the island, maybe even Mallory. Someone must have scuttled them, sunk them to the bottom of the sea.

There was no way off the island.

CHAPTER 3
THE COLD DARK

The wind coming in from the sea pushed at Shane. To his left, he heard it moaning. This was the source of the sounds that had plagued the island, and the wailing that sounded like lamentable things underground. The path he was on, where the ghost had vanished, led to a cave set into the rock.

From where he stood, Shane heard the wind winding through the cavern. There must have been more around the island, channeling the wind through narrow passages. This close, the sound was like listening to a dying man. It was low and mournful. It sounded like a hand would reach from the darkness of the cave at any moment, shaking as the last breath escaped from the lungs of some poor, desperate thing.

Shane looked back the way he had just come, the precarious and slippery path up the almost invisible ledge to the surface of the island. The smart move on his part would be to get Frank. The two of them could form a plan, investigate the cave system together, and see what was down there.

There were no boats, but if they found the King's lair, maybe they could put an end to the island's bloodlust. Maybe people would stay alive long enough for someone from the outside to reach them. They could build a signal fire and make it big enough for the smoke to be seen for miles. But they needed to live long enough to pull it off.

Shane looked at the cave's mouth, listening to the moan of the wind echoing through it. There was no guarantee it led to anything. It wasn't as though the ghost needed to hide there; they were no more held by rocks than they were by open doors. The cave could have led to a dead end.

There was no point in going to get Frank and have him come back to investigate what might have been nothing.

In an enclosed space, if there was danger in the cave, Shane was better suited to handle it on his own. Fighting in close quarters was easier for him than it would be for Frank, who only had his rings to rely on. The tight space would make Frank vulnerable to ghosts coming through the walls and would limit his ability to protect himself.

Shane headed toward the cave, keeping one hand on the wall as he stepped through the snow, probing with his boots before putting his full weight down to ensure there was a path beneath the surface.

Because of the angle of the cave and the stone overhang, almost no light entered it. Shane could only see a few feet in, and then everything was bathed in darkness. He pulled out his Zippo and lit it as he stepped forward, the howling wind causing the flame to dance in his hand and cast shadows.

The wind was less fierce inside the cave. Much of the stony exterior that hid the place from view protected the entrance, making it easier for Shane to light his way.

The passage within the cave was narrow, but still large enough for Shane to comfortably walk through. The rock was uneven, and he had to brace himself several times to stop from slipping on the uneven ground.

He moved slowly and cautiously, looking out for sudden drops or places where ice had formed that might cause him to slip.

The entrance was long behind Shane by the time something finally appeared on the path ahead. A form was slumped on the ground, propped up against the wall. He saw, even in the faint light of the Zippo, that it had once been a person. Now, it was just a skeletal body wrapped in rotten clothes.

Whoever it was had collapsed on the tunnel floor, leaning their head against the wall with arms and legs splayed out. There was no obvious cause of death, and no detectable trauma or blood on what remained of the shirt and pants, but the body had been there for a long time and was mostly just bones.

He crouched next to the corpse, looking it over for anything that might identify who it was or what had happened to them. Nothing much had survived the dampness of the cave aside from an oil lamp that sat next to the body, still half-full.

Shane opened the little glass door and pushed the Zippo inside, lighting the fabric wick in the lantern. He returned the lighter to his pocket and stood.

"Thanks," he said to the corpse, holding out the lantern. It was better able to fill the space with light, but there was still nothing to see. The ghost he had spotted outside had long since disappeared.

The ice soon gave way to slick dampness. The cave was insulated enough that the freezing temperatures outside did not penetrate it quite as badly. Shane's hand came away moist when he touched the wall, but the floor was still slippery enough that he needed to be careful.

It seemed like the tunnel might go all the way to the far side of the island as nothing new appeared, no branches and barely even any curves, until slowly, after more than twenty minutes of exploring, Shane detected something new in the air.

Beneath the sound of the moaning wind was something else. It was much softer like white noise. The deeper he went into the tunnel, the more pronounced it became, though it was by no means loud or very noticeable. Just a hushed, repetitive droning. The sound had a definite softness to it, a wetness, even.

Shane continued deeper, keeping the lantern raised as the hushed sound grew closer. It didn't raise in volume, it just became easier for him to hear.

The tunnel curved toward the island's center, and Shane followed it around a small bend. He watched as the light ahead of him spread out and was swallowed by an immense cavern. A small plateau overlooked the sunken floor of a cave about twenty times the size of the Great Hall up in the village. Shane stepped out into it, holding the lantern as high as he could, letting the yellow light bathe the cavern floor.

Endless movement filled the space. Here in the cavern, with the walls reflecting the sound, it drowned out the moaning of the wind. There was only the sloppy, slurping sound of eating and wriggling, slimy bodies writhing against one another.

The floor was covered in hundreds of them, blind and pale and dead. They were ghosts, as many as he had ever seen in one place. The cavern was too large, and it was too hard to see the far side, so he couldn't say for sure how many were there.

None of them responded to Shane's presence. He stood still and silent, watching as a layer of ruined, broken bodies squirmed and sloshed around together, glistening wetly and filling the space with the stomach-turning sound.

The spirits reminded Shane of the things he had seen stuck to the trees in the north. Not that they looked the same; the ones in the trees had been dried out in the sun. They looked almost mummified, their skin stretched over their bones like jerky.

Down in the cave, the ghosts he saw were almost the opposite. They were bloated, and their torn-up flesh hung in clumps as if the weight of it was pulling it loose. But they looked as though they had been torn to pieces. Many of them were missing one or more limbs. Parts of the flesh covering their torsos, chests, backs, and more looked like it had been shredded or pulled off. No tools were used here; everything looked savage.

The sound was a product of them writhing together, constantly crawling over one another as if searching for something. None seemed to be going anywhere, or even looking for anything. The movement seemed almost instinctual. Shane watched one climb across its brethren, get climbed over, and then repeated the process again and again, working in a circle with no clear goal.

The cave smelled sour, like bad meat. It didn't have the warm, wet rot of something trapped in a hot dumpster; this was more fermented, stale, and old.

Many faced Shane, but they were not seeing him. The ones that still had eyes were blind as bats, the eyes in their head either milky white or a rotten brownish-green color that wept a thick, muddy fluid.

The thing Shane had seen outside was one of these things, possibly the one that had pulled Brandon to his death. There was no way to know which one it was or if it had even truly seen him.

The sheer number of spirits was staggering. Hugh had explained to Shane that he had seen hundreds of people come to the island over the years, but nothing like this. For there to be this many ghosts, there had to have been thousands of dead on the island. The dead must have gone back centuries, well before America was even discovered by the Europeans.

Outside of a cemetery, Shane had never seen such a mass grave. War zones didn't have this many dead in one place. Someone had worked for a long time to build up the numbers. The Cannibal King was the logical answer, but he had to be older than Hugh suspected. Much older, and much more dangerous.

It wasn't impossible that everyone who had been to the island and died there had returned as a spirit. Shane would not have thought that at one time, but he had seen that there were ways to encourage a ghost to manifest after death. It involved pain and fear, and from what he had seen on the island, it was an ideal incubator for such things. But the numbers were so much more staggering than he had imagined.

The blind things didn't look like much of a challenge for Shane. The fact that they couldn't see him, and had no interest in him, meant that he could hold his own like he had against the ghosts from the trees. But the numbers were so overwhelming that if they all attacked at once, he couldn't overcome them. The village would be overrun in seconds if they surfaced. They needed to get everyone off the island, more than ever.

If the King controlled these blind creatures like he had the ones in the trees, he could send them against the living at any time. The fact that he hadn't yet was a puzzle, but Shane was not about to look a gift horse in the mouth. Instead, he began to slowly back away.

Blind though the ghosts may have been, he didn't know if they were deaf. The one on the surface had noticed him, so maybe some retained their senses. He didn't want to be seen down there, and he didn't want to draw their attention. Now, he needed to get back to Frank in the others.

Shane turned to leave. Some of the spirits had wriggled out of the cavern and into the tunnel, a pair huddled at the entrance, rutting around blindly. More had filtered into the tunnel.

He said nothing, watching them squirm across the tunnel floor. They were not moving quickly, and they kept their heads down. There was enough space to step over them as long as he was careful.

Shane moved toward the nearest one and lifted his leg. The ghost's head twitched, its milky eyes searching the air in front of its face, and a slimy, pruney hand lashed out and grabbed his ankle. The ghost screamed a wet and vomitous sound. The others in the cavern lifted their heads and joined it, shrieking as a chorus. Then, they began to lurch and slither toward him.

CHAPTER 4

CHANGING SEASONS

Shane instinctively pulled his leg free. The ghost had a poor grip; its sloppy, saggy flesh had no strength. The rancid, rubbery skin tore from the stress of Shane pulling away so quickly, peeling it from frail bones.

It continued to wail a deranged alarm. Frustrated, Shane raised his foot and stomped on the ghost's head. It burst like a melon, and the force of the ghost coming apart caused him to stumble back against the cave wall.

Others in the tunnel were crawling toward him, their saggy-fleshed hands clutching blindly at whatever they could grab. Shane kept quiet, not wanting to give them a target to search for, and kicked the heel of his boot into the face of the nearest one, crushing its bones.

The damage wasn't enough to destroy it, but it was crippled. The ghost crumpled, clutching its shattered head while Shane jumped over it, nearly falling on the slippery stone path waiting on the other side.

He kicked the final spirit out of his way, and it rolled with him, clutching at his legs as he passed. Several ragged fingers snagged in the cuff of his pants and nearly dropped him to his knees.

The oil lamp slipped from his grip, spilling on the ground. The splashed oil caught fire, illuminating his path and enraging the spirits, whose shrieking grew louder as the flame flickered in the dark.

Shane ignored the fire as he kicked back, freeing himself from the ghost and stumbling forward. His hands hit cold, wet stone but prevented a worse fall, and he quickly got back to his feet.

Behind him, dozens of the wriggling, moaning things had approached the tunnel entrance and were clawing toward him. Hundreds more kept pace, their horrible sounds reaching his ears as he pushed off the tunnel wall and ran through the dark.

The entire cavern was alerted to his presence now, and the floor, like a writhing mass of loose skin, surged in his direction. Hundreds upon hundreds of them were now focused on Shane, moving and churning mindlessly.

The path ahead of Shane was easy enough to follow in the dark, as the wind blew in from outside and acted like a beacon to follow in his blindness. He had to be more cautious now, keeping his hands on the walls for stability, but he could run and outpace the ghosts that followed him. None moved with any speed, and he heard them falling farther and farther behind as he fled.

Shane's chief concern was not just escaping from the ghosts but ensuring they would not follow him. He couldn't risk them getting to the village. There was no place else for the people to hide, no place they could go where they wouldn't freeze to death before they found a way to leave the island. He couldn't allow an army of the dead to follow him, which meant he couldn't return to the village. Doing so would leave a trail in the snow for them to follow, assuming they didn't already know where it was.

There was no way to know how intently the ghosts would pursue him. Realistically, they could follow him until he had passed beyond the mile radius that kept them attached to their haunted items. There was no reason for a ghost to grow tired or lose interest. Given where they were located, the village was within range. He could run them north to keep them away, but that was still a risk. And that was only if they pursued. Blind as they were, his hope was that they would give up when they could no longer sense him.

He cursed as the light from the tunnel opening appeared ahead. He still heard the wet, mealy grinding of ghosts crawling through the tunnel after him. They were not giving up so easily.

Shane ran out into the snow on the rocky plateau that curved up into the narrow path, invisible from the island's surface. There was nowhere to go but up, but he needed to be careful and fast when it came to deciding his next moves.

The ice underfoot forced him to slow and take more care. He couldn't risk falling off the edge of the cliff face. Once outside, he no longer heard the ghosts. The snow still swirled around the island, and the wind howled in his ears and echoed through the cavern. The wet, disgusting sounds of the dead were swallowed by it.

Shane looked back briefly and saw nothing. He had a reasonable headstart on the ghost as he found the path and climbed it, pulling himself back up to the snow-covered grass of the main island.

The tracks from earlier were all but gone. Where Frank and Clint had left to return to the village was barely noticeable. Shane decided he would not risk following them. Instead, he hugged the wall and continued to the north and east, circling wide of the others. The going was slow, the snow deep and heavy, dragging his boots and pushing against his legs. But he continued to forge a path away from Frank and the village toward absolutely nothing.

"Looks like it's letting up," Clint said, almost as a question.

The taller man peered out one of the windows in the Great Hall. Frank was not concerned with the weather because he had no control over it. Lamenting the storm didn't do anything, it was just a distraction from bigger issues.

Shane had been gone for a significant time. He had to have found something, Frank thought. There was no way he would be gone for so long if he was just idly looking and hadn't discovered the boats. But it was just as likely that what Shane discovered wasn't boats. He could have run afoul of the ghost from the forest, the Cannibal King. Or he could have reconnected with Hugh Carson. Or something else Frank couldn't even speculate about.

Frank had learned some years ago not to waste too much time wondering about things when he didn't have all the information. A person could drive themselves crazy pondering infinite possibilities when they didn't know what was happening. In the end, it proved useless to do such things.

More significantly, he knew not to worry about what Shane Ryan did. No one in the world was more capable when it came to dealing with the dead. If Shane was out doing something, it was for good reason. Even if Frank sometimes felt like an afterthought, he knew Shane had his reasons for doing what he did. Frank's work was no less important. He was saving people's lives. He had to keep them alive until Shane returned with word of the boats.

"Frank, the storm is really dying." Clint was more urgent this time.

Frank had been discussing with some of the elders the best way to organize everyone when they left. He wanted them to feel empowered like they were still in control of something since their lives had just unraveled so badly. Mallory had been a strong influence over everyone.

From what Frank understood, she was an intelligent woman. She often had good intentions, but Frank was all too familiar with people who seemed good outwardly, who did good things and helped others for most of their lives. But that little leftover bit, that darkness, it ruined everything.

In Frank's experience, no one was wholly evil, but few people were also wholly good. Mallory had let the darkness get the best of her, and she had done so willingly. She fed it, literally, and innocent people paid the price. But those she left behind were so used to her influence that they weren't sure what to do without her. Frank wanted to be there to guide them, but also to let them feel like they were doing things for themselves. They needed autonomy and confidence to get things done. They needed to know they could run things on their own.

Everyone was shocked to hear that Brandon was gone after such a short trip. Clint took the lead in explaining that the other man had slipped off the ledge and fallen into the sea, and that he and Frank had returned to avoid any further danger while Shane continued the search.

It was just one hit after another for the people of Maple Grove. They had lost so much, and so quickly. All things being equal, Frank was impressed with how well most of them were holding up.

"That's good." Frank was not really paying attention to the man.

"No, you need to look." Clint came toward him. "It's weird."

"Weird?" Frank asked.

He got to his feet and followed Clint to the window. In Frank's experience, the weather rarely qualified as something weird, and the storm dying down didn't meet the criteria. If anything, it was a relief. Not weird.

Frank approached the window. The panels of glass were thin and not particularly clean. There had been very little to see outside before. The Great Hall faced one of the old, wooden cabins. Aside from that, there was snow as far as the eye could see.

The way the village had been constructed in the bowl-like depression, it just filled with snow and ensured that everything looked white and forgettable aside from the handful of cabins. That was how it looked the last time Frank had been outside, when he returned with Clint from their short-lived adventure to the southeast corner of the island.

Frank stood next to Clint and looked out the window. The blasting snow of the blizzard was no more. A handful of fluffy, white flakes still drifted from the sky, but there was barely any wind to move them about. That would have not interested Frank so much if not for how the rest of the village looked.

He saw grass. The snow was scattered about in a light dusting.

Frank moved to the door and pulled it open, stepping out into the street in front of the Great Hall. It was not warm, but it was nowhere near as cold as it had been less than an hour earlier. The sky had cleared up considerably; there were only a handful of off-white clouds, and a bright sun shone down on the world.

"It's amazing," Clint said, joining him outside.

"Did Shane do this?" Alina asked, coming out as well. "Did he kill that other ghost you were talking about?"

"I don't know," Frank answered honestly.

The weather was tied to the island and the Cannibal King. Frank could not account for such a drastic and sudden change. Shane could have done something. Maybe he had been backed into a corner by the ghost and destroyed it in a fight. Frank was not willing to speculate on that, either.

He had experienced unexplainable things on the island, things beyond just seeing ghosts. Once, he and Shane had walked into the forest and found themselves far to the northwest out of nowhere. There was no way they could have been where they were, and yet, that was what happened. The fact that things on the island didn't make sense gave Frank pause.

The new weather could have been an illusion or a trick he didn't yet understand, but he was not about to complain. Less snow and no blizzard would make it that much easier when it came time to escape.

He just had to keep them all together.

CHAPTER 5

THE FREEDOM CONUNDRUM

The villagers filtered out of the Great Hall, as surprised as Frank to see what had happened. The milder temperature and missing snow were hard not to accept as a good omen. The blizzard had been oppressive and scary in the way that it had kept them trapped. But now, it looked like the island was opening to them again.

While most people were not nervous, Frank was a little suspicious. His nerves would be calmed when he talked to Shane again, to know for sure what had happened and that it was safe to leave. Until that happened, he needed to keep everyone wrangled. They were already wandering off, heading to their cabins or to visit those who had been isolated in their homes.

"We should head to the docks while we can," Lonnie suggested as a group gathered in the street.

"No." Frank turned to the others, regretting the finality in his voice. He didn't want to dictate. "We don't know where the boats are yet. And the docks are empty."

Someone else asked, "Can we at least go to our homes?"

Frank felt the tension building.

"Of course," he said. "Once Shane gets back, we'll all get together and figure out what happens next, okay?"

Some of the villagers left, happy to reconnect with friends or to return home. Others like Clint, Alina, and the men Shane and Frank had found at the sugar shack, stayed behind. They were the ones who had seen what they were up against and had no desire to be caught alone if the ghosts returned.

Frank headed back to the Great Hall, and Clint reluctantly followed. The others filtered in, eager to get warm and enjoy the false sense of security that the walls of the building provided.

"This is a good thing, isn't it?" Clint asked.

"It could be," Frank agreed, "but I won't know for sure until I can talk to Shane."

"But how can it be bad?" the other man wanted to know. "If this ghost wants to kill us, it wouldn't make the weather nice, would it? This has to be because Shane got rid of it, right?"

"Maybe," Frank said. "I don't know enough about your island to guess, Clint. There could be any number of reasons for this happening. I feel like it's a good thing, though. So, keep thinking those positive thoughts until we're ready to go, okay?"

"Okay." Clint sounded satisfied with that decision.

There was no sense making the man worry if he didn't have to. No one would get hurt if Clint felt positive about the future.

Frank fielded another round of questions from everyone who remained in the Great Hall about what would happen next. Nothing was different, but he was happy to go over the same ground he had twice before. Sometimes, in a crisis, people just needed reassurance.

Frank could do very little other than repeat himself. He didn't want to stare out a window like Clint, and he wasn't going to abandon the people of the village to go after Shane. His hands were tied, so he tried to seem useful and like he knew what was going on.

Frank listened to stories from everyone about their time on the island. Some told him about how they first discovered it, or their first year being there. He asked questions and kept the conversation going so people would feel involved but also distracted. The minutes ticked by, and he waited for Shane to return.

When the door opened, for a moment, Frank thought Shane had

come back. Instead, it was Lonnie. Frank hadn't even noticed that the man had left, but he was back now, and out of breath.

"They're at the docks." Lonnie bent over to rest his hands on his knees while he gulped in air. "I ran… all the way. The boats are there!"

Frank was on his feet and at the man's side, helping him to one of the benches so he could sit and compose himself.

"All three of them." Lonnie looked Frank in the eye. "I don't know what you saw, but all the boats are there."

Frank did not know what to say at first. What Lonnie said made no sense. He had seen that the boats were not there. All the men who took the boats were dead. It wasn't possible that they had returned.

"Are you sure you saw them? All three boats?"

"I went right down, Frank. I walked on the deck and tried to raise someone on the radio."

Frank ran a hand over his scalp. He couldn't account for how or why that would have happened, but it made him even more suspicious. Had the ghost brought the boats back? If so, why?

"Did you get anyone on the radio?" Clint asked.

"Nah, I don't know how to work the damn thing. Just static."

It occurred to Frank then that he might have been thinking of things the wrong way. His instinct was to believe the weather outside was a trick, and that the boats being back was something done by the ghost for some nefarious reason. But what if he was looking at it from the wrong angle?

The boats missing from the docks could have been the illusion. The storm could have been an illusion. Maybe the boats had never left. Maybe Blaine and the others had only taken them briefly and then brought them back. By the time Shane and Frank went to look, the island was obscuring them to make them think there was no way to escape. That certainly would have been much easier than someone finding a secret cove in which to hide the boats.

"You're sure they're real?" Frank asked.

Lonnie laughed and shook his head.

"Man, they're boats! How much more real could they be?"

Frank couldn't imagine that Lonnie could mistake anything for a boat, but he also knew Lonnie to be a bit of an idiot. There were just too many questions for him to take it at face value. He had to go see for himself.

"Clint, do you want to come with me to the docks?" he asked.

"Sure," the taller man agreed.

"Yeah, I'll show you." Lonnie got to his feet again.

Frank didn't want to make a production of it, but several others volunteered to go as well, including Alina. The hope he saw in everyone's eyes was hard to ignore.

"If Shane returns, let him know where we went, and that I'll be back soon," Frank said to those who stayed behind.

The others nodded, and Frank headed out into the village with a group of six others. The weather had improved again since he was out just a short time before. There was very little snow on the ground, and the sun was warm on his face. The niceness of everything, and the perfection of it all, made him more suspicious than ever. Still, if he could take advantage of it, he would.

They scaled the hill up and out of the village and then headed across the fields toward the western wall of the island. Snow had been two feet deep earlier that same day. Now, there were only isolated patches of it. The grass was wet and flattened, but it was there. It was green and alive. The journey was much faster than it would have been otherwise.

Frank looked at the maple forest to his right. He saw the sun glinting off the little aluminum buckets, and the snow there was all but gone as well. The trees were still devoid of leaves, still skeletal and spindly as they reached for the sky with thin branches, but nothing ominous moved among them. There was no sign of the Cannibal King or any other spirits.

There was palpable excitement from the villagers as they walked. Lonnie excitedly told everyone about not just the boats but how he was confident he could pilot one, having used a jon boat for fishing back in the day when he lived in South Carolina.

The trip to the western cliffs did not take very long, now that the weather was cooperating. When they reached the rocky path that zigzagged down the side of the stony wall to what waited below, Frank stood at the edge and looked down.

Just as Lonnie had said, the wooden dock stretched away from the shore and three boats were tied to it in the same position they had been when he and Shane had arrived several days earlier. It was as though nothing had happened, and the entire experience had been in his head.

"You see? I told you they were here! We should get everyone and go before any more of those monsters show up," Lonnie urged.

He was already eagerly making his way down the trail. Clint was caught up in the excitement as well, and even Alina was beaming, relieved to see the boats were there after having heard from Shane and Frank that they were missing.

Frank could not deny that it was a good feeling to see them and that the possibility of escape was within their grasp. They could leave the island behind, distance themselves from the Cannibal King, and put an end to the slaughter that had become such a common feature of Maple Grove Island.

He headed down the trail with the others, having to jog a bit to catch up with Clint and Alina at the back of the pack. The path weaved back and forth until they reached the bottom, and by the time Frank's feet were on the wooden dock, the others were on the boats as if they were leaving right away.

Frank approached the nearest of the vessels, a small cabin cruiser, and touched the edge of the fiberglass hull. It felt real; there was nothing illusory about it. Wherever the boats had gone, they had been brought back. They were real, they were solid, and they were ready to go.

"Are they functional?" Frank asked. "Do we have fuel?"

Nothing about the boats had changed since he had seen them. They even had the same junk piled on the decks that he remembered. One had a pair of gloves; another had a rope piled in a corner. Nothing had been moved.

Lonnie opened a storage compartment on the boat and pulled out two red Jerry cans that sloshed and were heavy in his grip.

"Two full fuel cans in here," he said.

"Keys?" Frank asked.

One of the other boats started, and Frank turned his head to see Clint waving at him from the second boat, the engine rumbling as it idled.

"Works good!" Clint yelled at him.

He turned off the engine, and Frank nodded. They had everything they needed. Except for the rest of the villagers and Shane.

"Okay," Frank said loudly, enough to get the attention of those on the other boats as well. "We should head back. Let everyone know the boats are here. They're functional, they're fueled, and they're ready to go."

Frank guessed that they could take maybe up to a dozen people on each trip back to the mainland between the three boats. Possibly more if they were willing to overload them a bit, but he didn't want to risk an accident. No matter how they divvied up the passengers, they would probably need three trips to get everyone off the island. And three people who were confident enough to pilot the boats through the rocks and back toward Maine.

Frank got off the boat, set foot on the dock, and looked back at the rock wall and its winding path back up to the island's surface. It was free from snow and as clean as it was the day Shane and he had arrived. He couldn't explain it. He hoped it was the result of Shane finishing what needed to be done.

He hoped it was finally over.

Chapter 6
Leave-Taking

It took Frank longer than he wanted to assemble everyone back at the Great Hall. Many people were happy to be back in their cabins, having made meals, and even started playing games with their friends. The people of Maple Grove were accustomed to their laidback lifestyle. They were not motivated to change much unless they absolutely needed to.

Once they had everyone in place, and they were certain no one was missing, Frank had everyone quiet down.

"Lonnie went to the docks earlier and discovered that all the boats have returned. We just came back, and I can confirm that they are there, they have fuel, and they are functional. We have everything we need to leave the island."

Excited murmurs rose from the others, and the drone of conversation took up almost instantly. Frank had to raise his hands and quiet everyone down again.

"As you know, these aren't large boats. With a pilot on each one, we can probably only risk taking twelve people back to the mainland at a time. Maybe, if we ditch some gear we don't need, we can get fifteen or sixteen in total. But I think we'll need three trips, so this will take a while, and some people will have to wait."

The prospect of having to wait for a trip didn't diminish anyone's excitement. Only days earlier, most of the populace of the island had been adamant that they would never leave. It was amazing what fear could do to people. Frank would rather not have used it as a motivator, but he was glad it worked. He had been unable to save Jackson Raines, but he could save the rest of them. That was some small consolation, though it would mean nothing to Jackson's father.

"How are they back?" one of the elders asked. People mumbled and nodded. That underlying suspicion was still there among some of them.

"I can't answer that," Frank said, "but this island—the spirits on this island—can make you see things. They could have been hiding them that way."

The explanation did little to satisfy anyone. Frank didn't have the time to explain to people how ghosts worked, how they could cast illusions, or make people see and hear things that weren't real.

"What matters is that they are back now. I checked them out myself. Clint started the motor on one. They're good to go."

"So why did it stop? Why would this ghost let us all go now?" the same person asked.

Frank shook his head, holding his hands out passively.

"I wish I had answers for you. My guess is that Shane found the ghost when he was looking for the boats. If he confronted it, and if he destroyed it, it would lose the power to keep casting these illusions. That could explain why the weather changed, and why the boats are back. But that's only a guess. We need to wait for Shane to come back to know for sure."

"You think he destroyed it? It's the last one, right?" Alina asked.

"That one was the most powerful," Frank answered.

People were already discussing the prospect of it. Frank was worried that the tenor of the conversation would soon change to, "If all the ghosts are gone, why bother leaving?" and he didn't want that to occur to anyone.

"Should we pack our things?"

"How much can we take with us?"

"When are we going to leave?"

"Who gets to go first?"

A dozen people had a dozen questions. Frank replied to them as best as he could. People talked over one another, and some offered answers.

Others just wanted to talk among themselves. Even if the weather had calmed down, the state of confusion among the people who lived in the village had not.

It was frustrating and disorganized, but it was a good distraction. Frank answered the questions one at a time, pointing out people to get them to speak up so everyone could hear. He just wanted everyone to participate, to feel like they were being heard, and to run out the clock. He could afford to give Shane a bit of time, but he hoped the other man returned soon. If he didn't, the villagers would get more frustrated, and Frank would have to come up with a new solution. He would also have to look for his friend if it came to that.

They were twenty questions deep when Clint, still stationed at the window behind Frank, rushed to the door of the hall.

"He's here!" the man exclaimed, heading outside.

Frank turned, intent on following Clint, but stopped as Shane Ryan stepped into the room.

"Shane," Frank said with a relieved smile. "We were going to send out a search party if you didn't come back soon."

Shane chuckled and shrugged, running a hand across his bald head.

"Wasn't as bad as all that," he said.

"I found the boats," Lonnie said like a child impressing his parents. Shane looked at him, raised an eyebrow, and nodded slowly.

"That so?" he said.

"I checked them out myself. Full of fuel, fully functional, right at the dock where we saw them when we got here," Frank said.

"How about that?" Shane said. "Guess that means we can go now."

"What happened?" Clint asked. "Frank thought maybe you found the King ghost and killed him or something. All the snow is gone. Everything's different now."

"Yeah, I saw that," Shane said.

He came into the Hall, glancing around, and then sat at the bench next to Frank, adjusting his coat and gloves before looking at everyone.

"I found a cave," he said, "on the other side of the island where I was. I went looking inside and I found where he lives. The King."

"You confronted him?" Frank asked.

"I did," Shane replied. "We fought, but I got him in the end. I thought we might still have trouble when I couldn't find the boats, but then you found them. So now everyone can leave."

He sounded excited, and some of the other people cheered. Lonnie clapped him on the back, and Shane smiled and nodded.

Frank ran a hand across his head, scratching the back of his neck.

"That was a big risk," he said. "Taking on the King alone. Was Hugh there?"

"No," Shane said. "It was a risk, but it was worth it. There's nothing left to worry about. And since you found the boats, we can leave any time now."

The villagers were excited, echoing his sentiment. Shane stood, and the others began to get ready.

"We still need to determine who gets to go in the first group and who stays behind—"

"We'll figure it out on the way," Shane interrupted. He was already on his way out the door.

Villagers rushed back to their homes to gather their possessions. Frank told everyone that they didn't have room to bring much with them, and they needed to be aware of the weight on the boats if everyone was going to get off the island as soon as they could. Even though they understood what the risks were and why they were leaving, it seemed like too many people were considering it a pleasure cruise rather than an evacuation.

Shane was leaving with Clint and some others, while Frank stayed behind and wrangled everyone to make sure they were all together. He didn't want stragglers in the village, potential targets for any of the other ghosts that might still linger on the island.

He watched Shane head out at the front of the pack and felt a curious sensation in the back of his mind. Like an itch he couldn't quite scratch, something seemed off. Shane had been very vague about the fight, and he almost seemed happy when everyone was eager to leave.

Frank would never go so far as to say that Shane was unhappy in general; he certainly wasn't miserable. But he also wasn't prone to many positive emotions. It had been a harrowing few days, and Frank felt relief that they could leave. Shane must have felt it much more acutely, especially after fighting with the Cannibal King.

There was no way that was an easy fight. The ghost was formidable and extremely dangerous. The fact that Shane survived was a testament to his strength, so he had earned the right to be relieved and happy to get off the island. But still, Frank couldn't shake the odd sensation.

He went from cabin to cabin through the village as the others filtered out slowly. He wanted everyone to go in a group, but that ship had already sailed. Instead, he ensured that no one was left behind and was the last one to leave the village, with Alina and a handful of others. Maple Grove was truly a ghost town now, and with any luck, no one would return.

By the time Frank caught up with everyone else, all the boats were filled, the tanks were fueled, and people had sorted themselves out. The first group was ready to return to the mainland, and the rest would remain on the docks to wait for the boats to return.

Clint would pilot the smallest boat, assuring Frank that he was confident enough to do so. Lonnie took the larger cabin cruiser, and that left a simple fishing boat with no captain.

"You can handle a boat, can't you?" Shane asked. He was waiting on the dock with the second and third groups.

"Probably," Frank said. "It's been a few years, but I'll manage."

"This first group here is all the older people, anyone who's sick or doesn't think they can wait for the second round. You take them back first, and I'll stay here with everyone else," Shane said.

"Right," Frank said.

Everyone else was getting settled. The people still on land sat down on the dock or waited among the rocks at the bottom of the path. Shane stood there, smiling at Frank.

"Everything okay?" Frank asked.

"Couldn't be better. Just relieved we can finally leave this place. I'll buy you a drink when we get back to land."

"Yeah," Frank said. "That sounds like a good idea. You sure you're okay waiting here?"

"Of course. The ghost is gone. Nothing left to worry about. You should get going."

Frank looked at the others waiting on the boats and nodded. They needed to get going. The way things had changed so quickly on the island, he didn't want to risk something taking a turn for the worse.

He untied the line and got onto the boat, started the engine, and then looked at the others. He waved to Lonnie and Clint, and they started out. The tiny inlet that led to the dock through the rocks was big enough for all three boats to go abreast several times over, but they took it single file. Frank knew there were hidden dangers beneath the surface, the same rocks that had gutted Hugh Carson's ship all those years ago, and probably dozens of others. Caution was key.

He looked back at the dock once they were underway. Most of the others were sitting, getting themselves comfortable for the long wait until the boats returned. Shane stood at the end of the wooden slats, inches away from the edge of the water, waving a hand over his head.

Clint waved back from his boat, and Alina waved as well. Frank only watched.

He had never known Shane Ryan to be the kind of man to wave goodbye.

CHAPTER 7
THE EMPTY COLD

The snow blasted Shane in the face. He had to keep his head down. No matter which direction he turned, if he was looking forward, the wind swirled and came directly at him. For once, he was thankful for a lack of facial hair, as he had nothing that could collect the snow and freeze it in place. Nevertheless, he kept his head down, glancing up only occasionally to make sure he knew where he was going.

He could neither see nor hear the ghosts behind him, not that such a thing proved anything. The spirits from the cave could have been ten feet behind him and he never would have noticed. The blizzard was worse than it had ever been, a total whiteout. There was nothing to see in any direction, just the snow in front of his feet and the faint hint of the eastern wall on his right side as he trudged onward in the ever-deepening drifts.

Shane kept his pace, almost marching, one foot in front of the other with a grim determination to put distance between himself and whatever might still be pursuing him. He needed to go north, away from the village and the others, to keep everyone as safe as he could. If the cave ghosts were pursuing, he'd have to devise a better plan, something more offensive, and put an end to things. But that was a bridge he could cross later.

It was hard to tell how much distance he had traveled given that he could barely see where he was. He only knew that his progress was slow. He kept the rocky wall to the east of the island in view, but the conditions made it difficult. He didn't want to venture too close, lest he put himself in danger of falling over the side. But when he got too far, it vanished.

He glanced up at one point, snow plastering across his face, and saw nothing out of the ordinary, so he pressed on. A handful of steps later, he was tumbling down an incline. For a moment, he thought he'd hit the cliff's edge somehow, that he was falling to the ocean below and certain death. Instead, he rolled through snow and came to a stop only a few yards from where he had started.

Shane lifted his head, shielding his eyes with his hands as he looked around. There were large shapes in the darkness. It didn't make sense, but he knew where he was. The shapes were cabins. He had fallen into the village. He should have been nowhere near it, but that was not how the island worked. It put you where it wanted you.

He looked back the way he had come and could not see any of the writhing, rotten ghosts following his trail. He quickly got to his feet and struggled to the nearest cabin. He wasn't sure whose it was, but he made his way around the side and threw the door open.

The interior of the cabin was cold. No fire was burning, nor did it look like there had been one in ages. The interior was gutted, devoid of tables, other furnishings, or possessions. Nothing. It looked like no one had ever lived there.

Shane left the cabin behind and turned back to the storm. It was so hard to make out the village, but some of the cabins were missing. None of the ramshackle ones were there, just the stone and wood cabins. The oldest ones.

He pushed deeper into the village, down the makeshift streets, but he could not find the Great Hall. Neither it nor the greenhouse was there. He was not in the village as it was, he was in it as it had been years ago.

No one was in any of the cabins. Not Frank or any of the villagers, and no sign that they had ever been there. It looked like it had been abandoned for years. There were a handful of scattered supplies, some firewood, a stray blanket, and an old cup, but nothing recent.

Shane ran his hand across one of the stone walls of an empty cabin. The illusion looked perfect. It looked like he was in the village, and it felt like he was in the village. The island was immaculate in its ability to deceive.

He thought of his home, the house on Berkley Street. A person could walk down a hall on the second floor, open the door, and find themselves in a hall on the third floor. It was not an illusion when it happened. The house could rearrange itself. It was not fakery; it somehow manipulated reality.

Shane wondered if that's what he was experiencing. Maybe the cabin looked and felt real to him because it was real. Somehow, the island had made this village different from the village where Frank was. For all Shane knew, he was in a different part of the island than he thought. Perhaps he was deep in the north now, transported to the far side of the island but hidden in the storm so he had no idea.

Something in the stone cabin behind him groaned, and Shane turned to see one of the maggot-like, writhing corpses making its way out of the corner, where a bed would normally have been placed.

The ghost had no legs, and some of its fingers were missing, but it still wriggled and clawed toward him like he was a flame drawing in moths. There were no eyes in the ghost's skull, just empty, glistening pits surrounded by sagging, bloated flesh. The mouth hung open, slack on one side, and the fat lips looked like the weight of them might peel away from the face at any moment. Every part of it glistened, looking puffy and ready to burst. It spoke of pain and anguish. The torture that the soul who became that ghost must have gone through would have been incredible. And the fact that there were so many of them...

Shane wondered how the King had done it. Drowning seemed obvious, but in such great numbers? Maybe they were victims of the island and not the King. Maybe these were the people whose ships had been dashed on the rocks, and whose bodies were still lost in the murky depths around the treacherous cliffs of Maple Grove.

Shane sneered at the spirit and saved it the trouble of struggling toward him. He crossed the room and lifted his foot, swinging out with a powerful kick. The ghost's head fell apart under the force, shattering like it was made of the thinnest glass.

The body burst along with the head, and the paltry rush of energy barely stirred Shane. It was gone, vanished from existence for only a fraction of a second before another of the spirits crawled free from the wall, and then another.

Shane had expected as much. The ghosts were mindless, powerless things. Their strength was in their numbers, and the island knew that. Or the King knew that. Whoever was playing games with him. This was not to harm him; this was just to make him angry.

He turned to look outside. There were shapes atop the snow, barely visible in the swirling white. More of them were coming at him.

Of course they were, he thought.

Shane attacked the ones inside the cabin. The first, he crushed by stomping its head, and the second, he took out with another kick. By the time they were gone, four more wriggled into the cabin, and more came after them, passing through the walls like water leaking through cracks.

It was easier to maneuver around the cabin with no furnishings, but the space was still small. Outside would not be an option, though. The snow was too deep, and the ghosts could hide in it. He had to stay in the cabin and fight them there, where he had cover from the weather and there was no place for anything to hide and surprise him.

He took them on as they came, kicking the heads from their shoulders and moving quickly to the nearest one, not letting them get the chance to come at him more than one at a time. But even as he succeeded in destroying the first four, the cabin flooded with more of them. Four became eight, and as he fought those off, the numbers increased to ten and then twelve.

There was no grace in the way Shane fought. There was barely even strategy. It was an abject slaughter, just ugly, dirty fighting for the sake of achieving the most damage in the shortest amount of time. The ghosts were too fragile to withstand the onslaught, but their numbers continued to grow as the space in which Shane had to work grew smaller and smaller.

He found himself surrounded soon enough, fighting from within a circle of open floor as the ghosts piled up, crawling across one another to reach him.

He kicked out at one as another grabbed his ankle from behind. His attacks became defensive instead of offensive as he kept the ghosts away. No longer was he trying to remove their heads; he was stopping their hands from sinking in. And still, they flooded in, three or four deep near the walls now, rolling toward him like an avalanche of drowned, rotten flesh.

A pair grabbed onto his left leg, while a third dug claws into his right. He swore loudly, turning and punching down through the top of one ghost's head. But the act of turning exposed himself on the other side, and he felt more hands clawing at his waist.

Shane struggled to keep his footing as more hands grabbed at him, pulling him down even as they climbed up his body. He could no longer kick; now, he simply swung his fists down. They dragged him to his knees and came for his face. He used fists and elbows, swinging, dropping, punching, in some cases even just tossing them aside when they got too close.

He felt fingernails digging at the fabric of his pants or forcing their way into his winter jacket. If not for their weakness and the layers he had on to stay warm, they would have been raking through his flesh.

He swung when he could. He kicked back blindly, digging his heels into whatever was behind him until his legs were immobilized. When he could no longer stay on his knees, and when he could no longer pull his arms free, he head-butted whatever came close to him. His forehead smashed through sloppy, loose ghost flesh and crushed the skull of the nearest spirit, destroying it instantly. The next one that came at him, he leaned in and sank his teeth into its rubbery throat, biting out a chunk of something sour and gelatinous before spitting it aside.

Shane felt them on his back now. They weighed him down, pinning him to the floor. There were too many of them, and they continued to moan and wail as more piled in, their weight building on top of him until he was smothered and couldn't move anymore.

Until all he could do was wait for death.

CHAPTER 8
ISOLATION

Shane took in a deep breath and felt the cool floor on his cheek. The pressure on his lungs vanished. Just a moment earlier, his body had felt like it was being crushed. As though he was pressed under hundreds upon hundreds of pounds. As though the ghosts had stacked themselves to the ceiling of the cabin. He had expected that they would bite or claw him to death, not smother him under their mass. In the end, he could do nothing but endure for as long as he could. He wasn't sure how long it was before he blacked out. And now, he was free.

He rolled over and stared up at the wooden planks. The cabin was empty. He sat up quickly and looked around. Not a single ghost remained. They had him, and they could have killed him, but they had done nothing.

A quick movement near the still-open door caught his attention. A shadow, just a glimpse of one, moving from the corner of his eye. Nothing remained when he looked, but it was not one of the ghosts. It was not low to the ground, it was standing upright, and tall. Shane couldn't say for sure whether he had seen antlers, but it didn't matter. Someone was still playing games.

He got to his feet. Part of him wanted to head out into the blizzard again, to scour the island for Frank and the others. He couldn't be in the same village. He had to be somewhere else, something the island had arranged for him. But if the island was in control of where he was and what he was doing, heading back out into the storm would just put him back in danger. And maybe that was all it wanted.

If the island was playing a game, Shane felt there was one simple solution that would deal with it better than any other. He would not play.

Shane headed outside. The snow was still falling, but not as fiercely. He went from cabin to cabin gathering supplies from the meager things that were left over. Some cabins had piles of wood. He retrieved a pair of dusty blankets and even found a hatchet. There was nothing extremely useful, and no food anywhere, but he could still get water from melted snow, and he had a couple of pots. He collected what he could find and brought it to the cabin that had once belonged to Mallory.

He used the hatchet to trim some of the wood, shaving off thin, dry pieces to make tinder and then lighting it with his Zippo to start a fire. It was a slow process to warm the cabin, but sitting near it helped get the chill from his bones.

Shane kept his head on a swivel. There was no sign of the ghosts, but he was wary they would return. He was obviously being tormented. Something wanted to see how he would react, but the game would only play out for so long. At some point, the island or the King would have their fill and kill him. He needed to be ready for that moment.

There was enough wood among the cabins to ensure that he could keep a fire raging for days. He ventured out once to fill a pot with snow and warmed it to drink. Beyond that, he waited. Huddled near the fire with blankets, he wanted to see what the island would do when he refused to engage. He was certain that it would eventually grow restless. Maybe it would send the ghosts again.

Shane had put the iron rings back on his fingers. Although the ghosts were easy to destroy, the numbers had proven his theory correct. He could not fight so many. But with iron, he didn't need to. One touch and they would be gone. It didn't matter how many there were at that point; they would get the advantage over him, and he'd still be able to use his boots to crush their skulls if it came to that. The island, or the King, needed a new plan.

The day stretched on uneventfully. Shane fed the fire with logs and drank water. After several hours, he carved one of the logs down with the dull hatchet blade. It took too much time, but he seemed to have plenty to spare. In the end, he made himself a rough, angular wooden ball. Once it was done, he leaned against the stone wall, the blanket insulating his back, and threw the ball into the air before catching it. Over and over, just something to keep his mind busy.

Shadows outside grew long. The wind howled, and the afternoon slipped into the evening. Shane took occasional walks around the village to see if anyone had returned, though he did not expect that to be the case. There were no tracks anywhere, and no sign of Frank or the others. By the time the sun started to set, he gave up on his walks and stayed indoors. He would wait the night out and see what the island thought of that.

Night came, and the wind outside died down. Shane was in a silent darkness, with only the crackling of the fire to keep him company. He occasionally looked out the small window, but only the firelight reflected back at him. When he stood up close to the window and used his hands to shield his view, all that waited outside was the night. The sky was covered with clouds, and there was no light anywhere. He couldn't even see the next cabin.

He was unsure what time it was. His watch had stopped working earlier, and he hadn't noticed. It was frozen like the world around him, perpetually stuck at a quarter past three. Surely it was past midnight, but it didn't matter.

Then something made a noise outside his door.

Shane turned his head, tense and ready to move. He looked at the door and listened. The fire crackled, and no other sound presented itself for a long, drawn-out moment. It sounded like a scrape, maybe. Not a knock, just something brushing against the wood.

Five minutes became ten became fifteen, and another sound came, this time on the far side of the cabin, on the wall adjacent to the fireplace. Closer to a knock this time. Something hitting the stones. A dull sound. A slap. Shane waited where he was. There was no need to investigate.

A short while later, the sounds became more frequent. The scraping sound of the door became a full knock, like someone pounding against it. Shane went to check only once and discovered nothing there and no tracks in the snow. Other knocks came on the walls and even the roof. Once, there was a tapping at the glass of the window, and he saw a flash of movement, a blur of something pale, but it was gone before he could focus.

He waited, listening and doing nothing, and new sounds joined in. Not just knocks but whispers. Voices came from the door and the window, filtering down the chimney into the fireplace. They were mostly unintelligible; even the language was uncertain. But other times, he made out this word or that.

"Dead," the voices said. "Flesh" at some times and "bones" at others. At one point, he was sure he heard his name.

Shane did not rise to the bait. He said and did nothing. The only time he exerted himself was to throw another log onto the fire.

Sometimes, there were long breaks between the sounds, and sometimes, they came in a flurry as though dozens of people were outside, clambering to get inside.

Shane lay down on the floor and threw his ball above his head. He ignored the ghosts outside, or whatever they might have been. He threw more logs on the fire. He drank more water.

He thought of what he would do in the morning. Much of his plan would depend on how the island reacted, how the weather worked, and even the layout of the world. If he was in the real village, Frank and the others had moved. The only other building he had ever seen was the sugar shack. Regardless of what had happened, it made sense to go there in the light and see if anyone was there.

If he could not find Frank and the others, if he was alone on the island with no way off, then he would go back to his original plan. He would find the Cannibal King and would destroy him.

"Shane."

The voice was slightly muffled. Shane thought he recognized it. Not Frank, not anyone from the island. He thought it was Jacinta's voice.

He sighed and sat up, leaning against the wall as he reached into his coat and pulled out one of his last cigarettes. Smoke filled his lungs as he inhaled deeply and blew it out across the room. There was a light knock at the door.

"Shane, let me in," she said.

He laughed softly.

That was a good one, he thought. He hadn't seen that coming. But he didn't move. One of two things would happen if he got up and opened the door. Either there would be nothing there, or there would be something there. He didn't need either.

The voice continued to call for him. Not frequently. Shane guessed that sometimes as much as an hour passed between its knocks. But it called for him again, and it was her voice. Sometimes, other voices said other things. He simply sat and waited for dawn.

He lost track of how many times in a row he caught the ball. He must have been doing it for five hours. He even managed to get some sleep until something knocked again. He was certain that it had come from inside the cabin rather than outside, but of course, nothing was there when he opened his eyes. Just the darkness in the windows and a nearly extinguished fire that he had to stoke and add more logs to.

No light crept in the windows. Dawn should have come, but it had not. Not only was he in a manipulated space, he was in a manipulated time. Whether or not the village was real, it was stuck in the night. The sun was not coming to help him on his journey to the sugar shack. It seemed as though the island had him where it wanted him.

"Come outside, Shane," Jacinta said.

Shane sighed again and reached into his pocket. He was out of cigarettes. He tossed the old pack into the fire and watched it burn.

"Come outside."

It was her voice but deeper and distorted. An angry, dark version of it. He looked at the door.

"If I come outside, we are going to have words," he said.

Laughter answered him. Not Jacinta but something masculine. It was deep and ominous. Shane grunted as he got to his feet, stretching after the discomfort of falling asleep sitting up against a stone wall. He put another log on the fire and folded up the blanket he had used, making sure everything was neat and ready in case he came back. He didn't think he would, but there was a chance.

"Alright then." He approached the door and adjusted the rings on his fingers. "Let's see what's so funny."

CHAPTER 9
RETURNING

It took longer than Frank had anticipated to offload everyone once they reached the dock in Spruce Head. The villagers were more than happy to get off the boats, but the problem was that no one knew where to go. Few of the residents of Maple Grove had any contact with the mainland. Part of the reason they were on the island in the first place was that nothing tied them to the world anymore. No homes, no families, and nothing they could go back to.

The people of Maple Grove were adults, and they all should have been able to take care of themselves, but some had been removed from society for a long time. None had ever felt a part of society. Frank hadn't realized that it had been many years since several of them had even left the island. The world was a different place to them. There were things they didn't understand and didn't want to.

In some ways, Frank thought, it was like dropping off children for their first day of school. That was a patronizing way to think of it, but it was the closest thing that came to mind. How they could reacclimate to the world was something to deal with later, though. More people needed to get off the island, and he had little time to spare to get everyone sorted.

Frank arranged for most of them to go to a nearby diner. Very few people had money. Anything they made on the island was managed by Mallory, which Frank hadn't thought of until they landed. He paid what he could to ensure everyone had coffee and a little something to eat, and then returned to the boats with Lonnie and Clint.

Mo was not on the dock, and his boat was missing as well. Lonnie and

Clint went to get the boats ready while Frank stopped in to see the harbormaster.

"Is Mo coming back soon?" he asked.

The harbormaster was as sour and unhelpful as he had been when Shane and Frank had first arrived. He seemed deeply engrossed in a magazine which he put down loudly and sighed before looking up at Frank.

"What am I, his mother? If he's not here, he's not here."

"It's just that his boat is gone, so I assumed he had to check in, give a time or something?"

"Check in?" the irritable man scoffed. "Didn't I explain this to you a few days ago? I collect the fees. I make sure there's fuel in the pumps. I call the cops if someone is causing trouble. That's my job. Anything else is your problem, not mine."

"Of course," Frank said. "Sorry to bother you."

"People always say that instead of just not bothering you," the man pointed out, his head buried back in his magazine.

The man they had met at first was not there, and none of the locals were at their boats, so there was no one else for Frank to ask. He had tried to raise Mo on the radio during their trip to shore, but he was quickly told that the channel was for distress calls only. He didn't have another channel on which to find the man, so he went silent and listened, hoping that Mo would respond. He never did.

They no longer needed Mo's help, but Frank still wanted to let him know that things were okay now and apologize if they had missed him on the third day when he said he would show up.

Frank resolved to look for the boat captain later. He didn't have much time to spare, so he returned to his vessel and headed back out to the island with Clint and Lonnie.

Lonnie took the lead and set an aggressive pace on the way back. Frank had encouraged him to be more cautious, especially given the dangers around the island hidden below the surface, but Lonnie did not easily follow directions or even listen to them. At least he was enthusiastic and on Frank's side this time. That was better than things had been when they met.

Frank's fears were unfounded, and Lonnie navigated through the rocks with no problems. They returned to the dock and the remainder of the villagers who waited there for them. Everyone gathered excitedly as they saw the boats returning, and Shane appeared to be right where Frank had left him, standing on the edge of the wooden platform.

There was no way to get everyone in on a second trip. They would have to come back a third time, but Frank got off the boat nonetheless to have a quick conversation with Shane.

"I had no luck finding Mo on the mainland. His boat is out, and the harbormaster was about as helpful as you'd expect."

"That sounds fine," Shane said. "Everyone here is eager to get going."

"Yeah, seems like it," Frank said. "So, everything was good while we were gone? No more issues?"

"Everything was fine." Shane confirmed.

The men stared at one another, and Shane smiled. Frank smiled back, looking cool and casual and friendly. Inside, his stomach was twisting in knots. He did not know who or what he was looking at, but he knew it was not Shane. He couldn't tell if the ghost had taken possession of Shane or if it was something else, but this was not his friend. Everything about him was just slightly wrong.

The others from the island might not have noticed. They didn't know Shane well enough, but Frank couldn't help the overwhelming sense of unease even just looking at the other man. The way he held himself was wrong. The smile on his face was wrong. Shane never smiled for no reason. He didn't make useless, fluffy small talk.

What concerned Frank the most was that he couldn't tell what he was looking at. Because it looked like Shane.

Frank spun one of the rings on his finger while they talked, idly using his thumb to rotate it full circle.

How hard would it be, he wondered. What's the worst that could happen if he reached out and touched Shane? If he pressed the iron to Shane's body, what would happen?

Frank was not sure how a possession worked. Would it force the ghost out of him? He didn't think so. But maybe something else was going on that Frank didn't understand. The way the weather had changed, the sudden reappearance of the boats, he couldn't claim with any certainty that he knew what was happening.

What if Shane was an illusion? Frank had never seen anything like that from a ghost. But he had never seen anything like what they had experienced on Maple Grove, either.

The other thing that Frank did not understand was that the thing that looked like Shane was helping them get off the island. Did that make it a friend like Hugh Carson? If it was something escaping the island and using Shane to hitch a ride, it would have left on the first boats.

Frank was confused, he did not have enough information, and he did not want to tip his hand this early. He nodded when the thing that looked like Shane made points and answered questions when asked. The conversation with shallow, surface-level nonsense that might as well have been talk about the weather. But Frank played it like it was a conversation he would have had with Shane any day of the week.

"You should get going," the Shane thing said. "Just one trip left, and everyone can go home."

"Yeah, bet you're relieved," Frank said. "Probably miss your family."

The Shane thing looked at him, and his smile grew slightly wider.

"Of course I do," he replied. "Who wouldn't?"

"Yeah," Frank agreed with a smile. "Who wouldn't?"

They held their shared look for a bit longer. Frank desperately wanted to call the thing out. Had he tipped it off with the family comment? Was that smile because it knew, or was it just playing along? And if Frank did call it out, how safe would everyone on the island be?

"We'll be back as soon as we can," Frank said.

He couldn't risk it yet. When he returned, when everyone was safely off the island, he and Shane would have a talk. He and this thing that wore his friend's face, spoke in his voice, and did a very bad impression of him. They would have a talk then.

"We'll be waiting," Shane said.

Frank divided the others properly among the boats to ensure the best weight distribution, the fastest and most efficient way for them to return to Maine.

"What happened out there, anyway?" he asked Shane. He needed to know before he left the remaining villagers with whatever the thing pretending to be Shane was.

"What do you mean?" Shane replied.

"With the King. Hugh was sure he would be impossible to defeat. How did you do it?"

"Oh, that was nothing," Shane said dismissively. "It wasn't that hard."

"But what happened?" Frank asked. "Were you able to corner him somehow? Did you take him by surprise? It must have been quite harrowing."

"I was scared at first, of course," Shane answered. Frank kept his expression blank, nodding slightly. "But I was able to overpower him. I crushed his head, the same way I did the others. That was all it took to kill him. He wasn't different from anyone else. And then, I realized everything had changed and we would be safe to leave, so I came back and found you."

"That's great," Frank said. "Promise me that you'll give me more details later. Maybe over a drink or something. I bet it's a good story. I bet everyone back home would love to hear."

"I promise I will tell it to everyone," Shane replied. "Now you should really get going."

"Can't argue with that," Frank said. "We need to make sure everybody's out of here before the weather turns again."

"Definitely," Shane agreed. "I'll keep everyone here safe until you're back. Then we can all be free."

"All of us," Frank said. "I'll see you then."

He turned his back and felt a chill run through him. It was difficult to turn around calmly the way he would have if Shane was really there, and trust that the thing wouldn't do something behind him. But he had to make sure it knew that he didn't suspect anything. For the safety of everyone else being left behind.

Frank untied the line that held the boat steady and tossed it to one of the villagers on the boat. He got on board and turned back just once. Shane was right there, right at the edge of the dock, right next to the boat. Frank hadn't heard him approach, and he was briefly stunned to see that they were only inches away from each other.

"Safe trip," the Shane thing said.

"Thanks," Frank replied.

Once more, Frank waited for Lonnie to take the lead, pulling away from the dock and heading down the inlet to the open sea. Clint followed on the smallest boat, and Frank took up the rear, allowing him to keep an eye on everyone during their voyage. Shane waved goodbye again, and the last few residents of Maple Grove Island took their seats to wait for the final ferry to the mainland.

Frank offered a friendly wave back. He was not looking forward to fighting whatever it was that looked like Shane.

CHAPTER 10
THE WAY IT WAS

Shane threw open the cabin door, his free hand balled into a fist and ready to strike whatever was waiting. Part of him suspected nothing would be there, that the island would continue playing with him and tormenting him. But if nothing else, he wanted to let it know that he was not afraid. If it was trying to unnerve him, it would have to try a lot harder.

Hugh Carson stood on the other side of the door, looking surprised to see Shane. No less surprised than Shane was to find the ghost. Despite missing a large portion of the flesh and muscle on his face, he could still display shock when something unexpected happened.

"You're here," the ghost said, almost asking a question.

"Apparently," Shane replied. "I'm not entirely sure where *here* is, though."

Shane stepped back from the door and Hugh entered the cabin. The wind outside still blew enough to ensure an unneeded chill would settle into the cabin if he left the door open, so he closed it behind the ghost.

"I take it that wasn't you knocking on the door earlier, or the windows, or the roof?"

"I only just arrived," Hugh said. "Where did the other cabins go?"

"Your guess is as good as mine. I thought this might be a different place."

"This is the village," Hugh confirmed, "but it looks the way it did when I arrived. These are the old cabins, still in that unused condition from so long ago. Where is everyone else?"

"You're asking the wrong man," Shane said. "I went looking for the boats and found some more ghosts in an underground cavern. Hundreds of them, more than I have seen in a long time. I was throwing them off my trail to make sure they couldn't come here, and then I ended up in this place. I thought it might be a trick, something constructed for my benefit, and that the others were still in the village waiting to leave."

"There is nothing left on this island," Hugh confirmed. "The other buildings are gone. The place you called the sugar shack is gone. The forest has greatly expanded. The island hasn't looked like this in more than a century."

"Great," Shane muttered. "And I'm out of cigarettes."

"I did not find the King." Hugh approached the fire and stared at it. "The forest is too different now. Things are not where they should be. And I feel that perhaps, he knows I was looking and does not want to be found."

"Why?" Shane asked.

Hugh looked at him, a question in his eyes.

"Why do you think he doesn't want to be found?" Shane clarified.

"With the others gone, he should have free rein. There should be no reason for him to remain hidden, and yet, I found no sign of him. I assume that is intentional. He has a reason for remaining out of sight, and he does not want to be seen right now."

"So, you think he is scheming some plan?"

"That was not my thought," Hugh answered.

"Then what?"

"As I said, this *is* the village. There are no people left on this island. If they didn't leave on the boats, everyone had to go somewhere. I was speculating that the King had captured everyone. That many living people would keep him busy for some time. He can be very patient in his cruelty."

Shane grunted. That was a possibility. Maybe the ghosts he found in the cave were there just to keep him busy long enough to let the King swoop in and do what he wanted. Frank would have put up a fight, but

Shane did not think he would have been very successful against the antlered ghost. This was not something to be defeated with iron rings alone.

"You think they could still be alive?" Shane asked.

"Some of them," Hugh said, "if that is what happened. But I am only speculating."

"Where are they then?" Shane asked.

The ghost shrugged.

"If I knew where to look, I already would have done so."

That made sense, but it was still frustrating. That this ghost could do as he pleased on the island but could still hide itself was not something Shane wanted to deal with. He wanted to bring the fight to the King. To end things rather than keep playing silly, drawn-out games.

"In all these years, you never saw where the King came from? Where the others kept him, aside from the north?" Shane asked.

"I never wanted to," Hugh admitted. "He left me alone, and I left him alone. When he rose, I stayed away. I let the others deal with it. Their numbers made the fight even. Less risk for me."

"Rose from where?" Shane asked.

Hugh looked at him unsurely.

"*Rose.* You said rose. No one rises from the north; they rise from below. Why that word?"

"I suppose I had seen the King escape from the others by going below the ground. They all hid in the earth and rose to claim the living."

"Where in the ground?" Shane asked. "What's down there?"

Hugh shook his head.

"I do not go underground. I never have."

Shane felt a twinge of frustration.

"This island is riddled with caves and tunnels, you know that, right? That sound, when the wind picks up? There are tunnels below us. I found a massive cavern in the southeast. There must be more."

"There are caves in the northern woods, but I have never ventured in. They are close to my travel limit. And, as I said, I don't—"

"You don't go underground, yeah," Shane finished for him.

Simultaneously acknowledging that he was looking for the King and not going to the place where it seemed obvious the King was located didn't make sense to Shane. If there are caves, you look in the caves. That seemed obvious.

"You are angry," Hugh observed. "You think I should have investigated underground."

"Not angry," Shane corrected. "I don't think I'm that emotionally invested in you, Hugh. But I am annoyed. I would have looked."

"The underground is where death comes from. The underground is where dead things go. It's where they're supposed to stay. I have been cursed to stay on this island for lifetimes. I might have to spend forever here. I might be on this rock until the seas boil and the sky turns black. But I can still hold on to the things that I believe. I can still refuse to tempt fate. I can still live, such as it is, the way I want. I will not walk into the devil's house and spit in his eye. I refuse."

"Loses some strength when the devil already ate off half your face," Shane said.

"Perhaps."

Hugh was annoyed, but Shane did not care.

"Did you know about the others underground? The cavern in the southeast, and whatever others might be around across the island? Do you know how many dead are here?"

"I told you already," Hugh answered. "A few hundred men have died on this island."

"There were more than that in the cavern alone," Shane said. "Many more. With you, and with the ones who were destroyed that we found posted on those trees, I'm starting to wonder how long this island has been taking lives. For that many to come back as ghosts, thousands must have died here."

The ghost seemed unaffected by the news, almost uninterested in it. After a moment, he shrugged again.

"I imagine people die all the time that I know nothing about."

"You're missing the bigger picture here, Hugh. This village, the fact the sun hasn't come up, and all the ghosts that are just teeming under our feet. This island is incredibly haunted."

"I do not think that escaped me," Hugh replied.

Shane held in a sigh that would have come out as a growl.

"I don't think you know what a haunting is."

"Has the definition changed in the past century?"

Something tapped on the door again outside. Hugh turned as though he meant to head toward it, and Shane waved him off.

"Don't bother. It's been happening all night."

"Nothing is there?" the ghost asked.

"No. Or maybe there is. Doesn't matter. Not a game I choose to play."

"If you want to find out where everyone is, should you not investigate things coming to your door?"

"This is all staged for me. Maybe for you now. It's theater. It's games. This is how a haunting works. The world changes for you, to torment you. A haunting isn't a ghost, it is the environment. It's the experience. And this island is very good at it. It can instantly change the physical world. That will not be easy to fight, and so I'm choosing to not engage."

Hugh grunted but nodded as though he understood.

"I suppose that makes sense. But is there not a flaw in your plan?"

Shane waited for him to continue, but he seemed like he had nothing more to add.

"Such as?"

"You have no food. The island is not alive. Even if the King leaves you alone and nothing comes in here to kill you, you're still eventually bound to die."

Hugh had a point, but Shane had never intended to stay in the cabin for that long. Now that he had a little more knowledge, now that he knew there was no sugar shack, and he seemed to be in a time-displaced version of the village, he could adapt a new plan.

Shane's obvious course of action seemed to be what Hugh did not want to do. They had to go underground and find the King where he lived. If Frank and the others were there, they needed to be rescued. And if they weren't, or if it was too late, the King still needed to be destroyed.

"If I'm going to die anyway, I have no reason to not fight the King, do I?" Shane asked.

Hugh chuckled wryly, his ruined mouth almost able to smile.

"So, either we stay here, and you die, or we venture out and you die. Either way, I end up trapped in a dark place that serves as a reminder of the night *I* died. You have backed us into a corner."

"Not me. And you don't have to come, but I am sick of this goddamn island. I will find those caves, and I will tear those antlers off that thing's head and shove them right down its throat."

"Or die in the process," Hugh countered.

"You like to gamble, Mr. Carson?" Shane replied.

Hugh laughed a surprising bark that sounded ragged and painful. Shane had not thought the ghost capable of laughter; he seemed too depressed for it.

"Your confidence is boundless. I will not let you die alone if you insist on doing this. I will watch you die."

Shane smiled. If the sun had no intention of rising, there was no reason to wait before they headed out.

"My confidence is only matched by your lack of it, Hugh," he said. "Let's go find a King and tear down his throne."

Shane made his way to the door, and Hugh followed him as he pulled it open. Outside was just snow and darkness. But there was a trail in the snow, one set of footprints that led from his door out of the village and toward the forest.

"That looks like an invitation," Hugh remarked.

"Yes, it does," Shane agreed.

He would not turn it down.

CHAPTER 11

THE MYSTERY MAN

Only two boats had to return to the island. There were not enough people left to require all three. Frank had Clint stay on the mainland. Frank had realized that Clint was a calming influence. Everyone liked him, even if they didn't listen to him all that often. He kept a positive attitude, and that was a good thing. Also, Frank didn't want him to return to the island.

Mo had still not returned. Frank didn't know what the man's workday was like. Maybe he spent hours on the water. Maybe Frank and Shane had just been lucky when they met up with him that first time. He didn't want to worry about it too much until he had a reason to.

It was a much faster turnaround time on the second trip. Things were more organized, and Frank knew where everyone needed to go. He had Clint lead them away from the harbor and then was back on the boat quickly, this time taking the lead with Lonnie behind him.

The day grew longer, but there was plenty of time before dark to get back to Maple Grove. Frank kept thinking of it as a simple plan. Take everyone on the boat, head back to the mainland. But he knew there was more to it than that. The confrontation with the thing pretending to be Shane would happen on this trip.

Frank wondered how best to approach it. There were still too many people for Lonnie to take everyone on his boat. Frank didn't want to strand anyone, but he couldn't very well take them and not the fake Shane as well if he planned to leave.

Frank was nervous. If it became a physical confrontation, he did not think he could challenge Shane. Not even something pretending to be him.

Shane's life was more violent than Frank's. Frank had been in combat, and he could hold his own, but he knew his limitations. And, just as importantly, if that really was Shane and was just possessed, he didn't want to fight his friend. If something was inside of Shane, he wanted to get it out. He wanted to help him.

Frank brought the boat in through the small inlet and returned to the same place he had docked previously. Shane was there waiting along with the handful of leftover villagers. The island was unchanged, the weather was pleasant, and the sky was mostly clear. Everything was the way it was when they had first arrived.

The last few people laughed in that tired, relieved way that people do when the thing they've been waiting for finally pays off. They joked among themselves and then split between the two boats after Lonnie pulled up to the dock. In moments, only Shane was left, standing on the wooden slat platform.

"Ready to go?" Frank asked.

"Yes," Shane answered.

He stepped off the dock and onto the boat. Frank felt an odd sense of relief when it happened. Part of him thought that Shane would attack once everyone was squared away.

It didn't make sense, of course. If Shane was going to kill Frank, he would have already done so. This Shane, whatever it was, wanted to leave with everyone else.

The fake Shane had helped organize everyone. It had been gracious, which was not a word Frank would normally use to describe Shane. But it had been a useful asset during the evacuation.

Frank struggled with the idea. Was it safe to take the thing that looked like Shane off the island? Would more people be in danger if he brought it back to the mainland?

Whatever it was could have left at any time. The boats were there. It didn't have to possess Shane; it could have possessed Blaine or Mallory or anyone. Something else was going on, and Frank couldn't wrap his head around it. He was cautious and nervous, but he didn't think the Shane thing would cause trouble. Yet.

The boat passed out of the inlet and into the open ocean. Frank stood at the wheel, with the boat's key attached to his wrist by a springy, plastic lanyard. Shane was with the others behind him, sitting on the bench seats and waiting for the ride to be over. He was like a tourist. Frank kept his eyes forward, not wanting to arouse suspicion. He was just doing his job. He was getting everyone to safety.

The wind picked up again once they were past the dangerous rocks. Nothing nearly as dramatic as it had been on the island, and nothing dangerous, but there was a real chill to it. It was colder than it had been all day.

Flakes of snow fell again. Frank was glad they had made it in the time they had. They had everyone off the island now, and if the poor weather was returning, they would only experience the beginning of it.

He played out different scenarios in his mind about what to do with Shane. Would they all go to the diner together? Would he stop him on the street? He would have to touch the Shane thing with some iron soon and see if anything happened. If nothing did, there would be a different sort of confrontation. Frank would have to stop being coy about it and address whatever it was directly.

The thing that looked like Shane had been amiable. The confrontation might not cause it to become violent. It might be cooperative. If it wasn't, Frank would cross that bridge when he came to it. He didn't like playacting, but for the sake of everyone else, it still seemed like the best idea.

The water grew choppier. Frank's experience with boats was limited, and he wasn't confident that he could navigate a storm well. The distance to the mainland wasn't great, but there were still miles to go. The wind pushed at the boat, rocking it slightly. It wasn't dangerous yet—the passengers hadn't even commented on it—but Frank felt it. He felt the boat shifting as he steered it, and he had to correct a little harder to handle the chop.

"Everything okay?"

Shane was at his side, and Frank nearly jumped. Again, he hadn't heard the man approach. Hadn't even seen him in his peripheral vision. It was like he was just there, out of nowhere. Frank didn't like that sensation, nor did he like the implication that this thing wearing Shane's face could just be wherever it wanted to be.

Frank was sure there had been nothing supernatural about Shane's approach. The others on the boat would have noticed if this thing had suddenly puffed from existence and reappeared elsewhere. He had probably just walked very quietly up behind Frank. It wasn't any less unnerving to have not sensed it until he was right there.

"Getting a little rough seas, but everything is fine," Frank replied. "You all good?"

"Everything's fine," Shane replied.

They stood next to each other in silence, with only the drone of the boat's engine filling in the gap behind them.

Shane placed the hand on Frank's shoulder. He flinched involuntarily, a barely perceptible motion. He regretted it immediately and felt awkward about it. The smile on Shane's face grew a little lighter.

"Looks like we got everyone off the island," Shane said, his hand still on Frank's shoulder.

"Yeah, looks that way," Frank agreed.

"No reason to ever go back."

Frank just looked at him, unsure of how to respond.

"There's no reason to ever go back, is there, Frank?"

His hand squeezed Frank's shoulder. It wasn't hard, but there was firmness and insistence. Frank's stomach twisted again. A feeling like the world had bottomed out, and he was just about to fall.

"No, I don't think so," Frank replied.

"Good," Shane said.

And then he was gone.

Frank blinked, and snow swirled out of a darkening sky, causing him to flinch again as wet flakes hit him in the face. The others on the boat reacted with cries of shock and surprise that they suddenly found themselves in the middle of heavy snowfall. The partially clear skies were now dark and gray like someone had flipped a switch. Sunshine and blue skies were gone. Gray skies extended for as far as Frank could see to the east, north, and south.

The villagers on the boat began to panic, asking what was happening as they held on tightly. The boat rocked more fiercely now, with the storm making the seas much rougher than they had been just a moment earlier. It was like they had been dropped out of the sky into a different ocean.

Shane was no longer on the boat. He had not fallen overboard; he had simply blinked out of existence.

Frank looked back toward the island, which was obscured by snowfall and distance. He wondered how far away they were. He guessed they had traveled about a mile from the island.

Frank cursed silently. Shane was not real. Not a possession, not a real thing. A ghost, maybe. Somehow making itself look just like his friend. Or something conjured up by the island. Frank didn't understand how that worked. He had felt the strength of Shane's hand on his shoulder. He smelled smoke on the man from cigarettes smoked in the past. Everything about it had been so real. If he hadn't known Shane, if he hadn't been able to pick out what was wrong, Frank never would have suspected.

Whatever it was had wanted Frank to leave. It was bargaining. It had traded everyone for Shane. It wanted to keep him there; that was very clear. There was no reason to go back to the island. But Frank had not agreed to those terms.

He pressed onward, pushing the boat as hard as he could, given the conditions. He didn't want to risk anyone's safety, but he needed to get back. He needed everyone off the boat, and he needed to turn around. He was not going to leave his friend in the hands of whatever controlled Maple Grove.

Once they were back at the harbor, Frank got everyone off the boat as quickly as he could. He offered an abrupt goodbye and asked Lonnie to make sure they got to the diner. The other man wanted to know what Frank was up to, and Frank told him he had a few things to finish up before he joined them.

He waited for them to head out of sight, and then headed into town to get some much needed supplies for his mission.

He needed to find Shane Ryan.

He just hoped he wasn't too late.

CHAPTER 12
THE NORTHERN WILDS

There were no longer any fields. The empty expanse of snow between the village and the maple forest was gone. It was just trees now. The forest was everywhere; it was everything on the island. There were no aluminum buckets collecting sap, either. This was true wildlands. This was the island the way it was when it started. When people first discovered it, Shane guessed.

"The landscape is different," Shane said.

"Clearly," Hugh replied.

Shane shook his head and grunted. They were in the woods, midway across what would have been the open field on the island as he knew it.

"Not like that," he said. "Look to the north there. That rise never existed before. And there's another one to the west. The topography of this place is all wrong."

"Lands change over time," Hugh said as something of an afterthought.

"Takes a long time to make hills come and go. This is meant to be confusing. Those are some specific details. This is a complicated arrangement. The control over this place is impressive, and that makes it dangerous."

"How much experience do you have with hauntings?"

"Enough," Shane answered.

The problem with the house in Nashua compared to the island was that his house rarely worked against him. As a child, when the girl in the pond was still there, things were different. Her influence affected the house and how it worked. But since Shane had claimed the property and destroyed the girl, and the spirits that remained in the house were less prone to fits of rage and murder, the house was not the same. Not to him, anyway.

The house was still a danger to outsiders. By that same token, the island was a danger to him. But the danger seemed exponentially worse on Maple Grove. It was unpredictable and powerful. He couldn't let that slip his mind. He couldn't take anything for granted.

He hoped the King operated in the same position as the girl in the pond had been in his home. Maybe not the conductor of the power that flowed through the haunted place, but certainly an influence. A locus of some kind. If he could be destroyed, the island could possibly become more docile and forgiving.

"I must admit, I am unsure of where to go," Hugh said. "If the landscape is truly changing, we could be wandering toward anything."

"There's something out there," Shane assured him. "Something waiting."

"One assumes. But you will eventually freeze to death."

"Thought I was going to starve to death," Shane countered.

"In the cabin. Out here, you will freeze first."

Shane had no response to that. There was so little interest in the ghost's voice. He wasn't being sarcastic or joking or threatening. It was an indifferent observation. He was simply confident that Shane was going to die one way or another. It was refreshing in a way. There was no bias. It was unusual to deal with a ghost who didn't have a vested interest in Shane living or dying. Most that he came across wanted one or the other to be the outcome.

They walked through the woods looking for anything familiar, any sort of indication that they were on the right track. There was a strange kind of familiarity to the place, but Shane couldn't say that he had been anywhere in that forest before. It was a forest. If you put a group of maple trees together anywhere in the world, they were probably going to look similar.

Hugh did not discuss it, but Shane sensed the ghost had the same dilemma. There was a feeling that they should recognize where they were, and he would get flashes of memory. He would get the inclination that if he turned right, there would be a ridge or a fork between two trees, and it never panned out. When he thought he was in a familiar place, nothing around it matched his memory.

Snow continued to fall, and the sky remained dark as night. Shane thought they had been walking for about two hours. It should have been getting close to early afternoon. Instead, it might as well have been midnight.

Hugh often took the lead, and it seemed at some points that he knew where he was headed until he soon became dissuaded when none of what he expected to see appeared. Eventually, they just walked for the sake of walking. If there was something to discover, they would discover it.

"This looks familiar," the ghost said as they entered a clearing in the trees. There was a ridge to the north, and Shane heard the nearby trickling of a stream.

"The graves," he said.

There should have been a circle of stones on the ground, the barely marked gravestones, or whatever they were, that the cannibals had always dragged their prey back to. Only now, the clearing was empty. There were no stones, just empty space under the snow.

Shane used his foot to kick some out of the way, poking at the hiding ground beneath. Not a single stone remained. Perhaps the forest they were in represented a time before they had been arranged here. Was the forest telling them something?

Hugh was about to say something when Shane felt the ground beneath his feet shift. The ghost must have sensed something as well, and the two of them simply looked at each other. The movement increased, and Shane put his hands out to stabilize himself. The ground was rumbling. It felt like an earthquake, and the sensation was growing.

As the shaking increased, a sound came with it. It vibrated through the earth and the trees, and into the air around them. It was a roar, a bellow of rage, a challenge from a predator. The King, somewhere, was howling in the deep parts of the earth.

It traveled through the same channels that carried the moaning of the wind during the storms. The island came alive with the sound of the enraged spirit. The island was screaming, seething, and rumbling over some unknown slight, or in some demonstration of power.

"He knows where we are," Hugh said.

"I assumed as much," Shane agreed.

Some of the trees at the edge of the clearing creaked ominously. Shane backed up as one of them leaned, and the forest filled with the sound of cracking wood. The tree fell over, its branches scraping against others, and took a smaller tree down with it.

Hugh did not need to move, but Shane only made it several steps before falling in the snow, unable to keep his footing due to the shaking of the earth and the slick surface he moved on.

He scrambled and rolled to get out of the way as the branches crashed into the clearing, narrowly missing being stabbed by one of them. More trees fell, and the sound of snapping wood went off like gunfire throughout the forest. When the next tree fell in the clearing, the ground itself split.

Shane pushed back again and watched the snow fall into a sinkhole. One of the trees tumbled in with it, all of it vanishing as a pile of dirt-encrusted roots upended and then was swallowed whole into the dark chasm.

The rend in the earth continued to expand like someone had dug their hands into the ground and was pulling it apart. A new sound overpowered the furious roar of the King, wherever he was. A wet, sloppy noise arose from the rift, and Shane cursed. He did not need to see what was waiting in the darkness to know what it was.

"There are dead men down there," Hugh said casually, looking over the edge of the abyss.

"That's what I found in the cave to the south," Shane told him, getting back to his feet and using a tree to steady himself.

No light came from the sky overhead, but there was an ambient light to the night, something even the clouds couldn't completely hide. Shane saw the glistening bodies in the chasm. They writhed and scrambled, clawing over one another up the sides of the hole. There was no way to tell how many were down there, but Shane bet it was in the hundreds.

"I cannot fight this many," Hugh pointed out.

"They're not strong," Shane told him. "They're like the ones from the trees. But they overwhelm."

Hugh looked at him, his ravaged face unsure.

"Are you suggesting we fight?"

"For now. Until we can't. The more we destroy, the fewer this place can send at us next time."

"Next time," Hugh said softly as the first of the bloated monstrosities emerged onto the surface.

"There will be a next time," Shane assured him.

The rage of the King was dying down, his point made. The earth rumbled beneath them with aftershocks, but the roar had subsided. Now only the slurping, squelching noises filled the night as the rancid ghosts clawed their way toward Shane.

The ghosts ignored Hugh. He might as well have been one of the trees for all they cared. It gave him an advantage that Shane hoped he appreciated.

"Help or don't." Shane slipped the iron rings from his fingers and put them back into his pockets. He didn't need them yet.

He pushed off the tree that was supporting him and came at the first of the ghosts, a thing with a face that looked like it was melting off, with lips like grey, rubbery worms and swollen, milk-white eyes.

The ghost reached out dumbly and blindly, swiping near Shane's leg but not with enough accuracy to make contact. Shane drove his fist down through the spirit's skull, crushing it.

His experience with the ghosts had taught him not to waste time. He knew that soon enough, they would surge out of the hole in numbers too great to handle, so the more he could get done now, the better.

Shane's elbow collided with the next ghost's jaw, breaking it off the spirit's skull. It crumbled and Shane was back on his feet a second later, kicking the rest of the head from its rotten shoulders.

Hugh was slow to join. He observed Shane take out a third ghost before finally wading in. He stepped among the spirits climbing from the rift and bent down, grabbing one by the head and twisting quickly and harshly. The fleshy neck crunched like old chicken bones before Hugh pulled off the head, stumbling when the ghost vanished with a limp burst of energy.

"They are like fabric worn so thin you can see the light through it," Hugh observed.

"Whatever works for you," Shane said, taking the head off another one and forcing a second back into the hole where it was lost in the churning of flesh.

The gap that had opened in the earth was about the size of a bus. And now, every inch of it was alive with movement. Ghosts climbed out around the hole; fifty had surfaced already. Shane continued dispatching them as quickly as he could. He was looking for efficiency: numbers only. He had eliminated nearly a dozen by the time they began to double up on their attacks, and he was forced to start moving back and go on the defense.

"How long are you able to continue this?" Hugh asked, pulling the head off another spirit.

"Was just thinking of changing things up," Shane replied.

He slipped his hands into his pockets and pulled out the iron rings. He'd hoped to have more time to fight, but a dozen ghosts gone was a dozen ghosts gone.

Shane took quick shots at the nearest ghosts, simple jabs to plant the iron rings into the meat of their ghostly flesh. They vanished in a blink.

"We should move," Shane suggested.

"Very well." Hugh lacked the urgency Shane felt. The ghosts weren't swarming out by the dozens for him.

They were all focused on Shane, and they kept coming.

CHAPTER 13
THE CURSED CREW

Sweat beaded on Shane's forehead, and he felt some running into his eyes. He ran as fast as he could with Hugh at his side, blindly through the woods toward anything that would get them away from the ghosts.

Other sinkholes had opened in the ground. The forest was riddled with them, and patches of the crawling, rotting spirits came for him from all directions. It was like running through a minefield, and he had to constantly change direction.

He took out several more as he ran. When the snow was not deep and he had mobility, he crushed the heads of those that drifted close or planted an iron ring in the back of their skulls. More were banished, and a half-dozen more were destroyed.

Even though they were still not entirely attacking Hugh, they seemed aware of his presence and avoided him. Self-preservation was something they seemed to understand. Their focus remained on Shane, though.

Even with the snow, Shane was faster than the ghosts. Getting away from them wasn't a problem; staying away from them was. They were just as prevalent in the woods as the trees, crawling, moaning, and grasping at him everywhere he went.

"There." Hugh pointed out a ridge ahead of them.

There was another open space where the forest dipped before it started up again and, from what Shane saw, no ghosts were there yet.

He followed the ghost's lead and took a left turn, unsure where he was even headed now. Snow crunched underfoot, and his breath steamed before his face, but his legs kept pumping. He wouldn't risk slowing down or taking a breather even when it seemed like none of the ghosts were around. He knew they were coming. They were relentless and didn't need to stop. They were like locusts. They would eventually catch up and swarm.

There was a familiarity to the ridge and the landscape ahead of them. Shane thought it might have been where Hugh had thrown him in one of their previous encounters, but some of the details were different. Maybe they were at a different place along the ridge, or it was because the forest was showing the way it looked long ago.

The ghost quickly went over the edge, not needing to be careful about his footing or what waited below. Shane paused at the top, looking for the easiest way down, and then skidded through snowy, half-frozen soil, and exposed roots, maintaining his footing until he got to the bottom maybe thirty feet below.

At the bottom of the ridge, Shane took a moment to orient himself. There was a swath of growth, shrubs, and other small plants, now mostly dried out, skeletal things lightly dusted with snow. The forest began again several yards beyond, but it was the best place he'd seen in a while to get a look around that wasn't obscured by maples.

There was no sign of the ghosts ahead, deeper in the woods. To the left and right, it was hard to say. The tree cover was dense on either side of the clearing, and the ones behind them would come soon, filtering down all over. Straight seemed to be the smartest and best way to go.

Hugh had stopped. Shane was about to yell at the ghost, tell him to get his bones in gear, when he saw why his companion stood still as though lost in thought.

To the right, around a pile of dirt and debris that had long ago slid down from the ridge, was an overturned tree. Shane recognized it right away. He had found it last time he had gone down the ridge. The bottom was hollowed out, and it had been full of skulls before. It was no longer full of skulls.

Several ghosts were huddled in the hollow under the tree. They were not the creatures from underground. They were not the mindless, ravenous things that pursued prey.

The ghosts had been eaten. They had been savaged like the ones Shane had already destroyed on Maple Grove. But many were still partially dressed, adorned in the blood-soaked, shredded scraps of whatever they had worn when they were torn apart and eaten.

Most of them wore simple garb, what looked to Shane like linen shirts or another light material stained with sweat, dirt, and blood most of all. Some still had on soft leather boots; some were missing feet entirely.

One man wore the remnants of a uniform Shane recognized from history books. It was military, British, from several hundred years ago. A naval officer's uniform. His shirt was missing, but he still had his coat on. The pant legs were torn, but they were still mostly attached. These men had once been sailors.

"Mr. Carson," the uniformed ghost said.

He was not a tall man, but Shane could not tell what he might have looked like. His face was ruined. The muscles of his jaw had been chewed to the bone. What little skin remained on his face was around his hairline.

The ghost had lost his ears, and now only mangled, bloody holes in his skull indicated where they were. It looked as though someone had peeled away his skin and muscle and left only blood-soaked bone. He had no face, just a glistening, blood-red skull.

"Mr. Wellesley?" Hugh said softly.

The bloody skull-faced ghost stepped from the tree's hollow as the others huddled behind. They watched with curiosity and hunger, at least those with enough face left to register expression. Few had eyes left, and though none were as badly savaged as Wellesley, most were missing large portions of the skin that had once covered their faces.

It was as though their killers had wanted to take their very identities. The rest of the bodies were like the others had been, like Hugh's, torn and eaten. But the faces were so much worse.

"Where have you been?" Wellesley asked.

The other ghosts whispered behind him. It was like a dry hissing, a raspy sound that brought no words to Shane's ears. Their speech was too ragged and garbled with their broken lipless mouths to make anything sound clear.

"Family reunion?" Shane asked.

Hugh didn't turn his head.

"This is my crew. Mr. Wellesley, Mr. Bundy, Mr. Lowell… everyone. Except I do not see Captain McKenzie."

The whispering grew silent, and the eyeless, bloody skull cocked very slightly to one side. Empty eye sockets stared at Hugh. Shane might as well have not been there. It was a complete one-eighty from the subterranean ghosts. These ones only had eyes for Hugh, despite having no eyes.

"McKenzie? Oh no, Mr. Carson. There is no more Captain McKenzie," Wellesley said.

The ghost's voice sounded wet and somehow dry at the same time, like someone with a chest cold. Shane saw, behind the collar of the jacket the ghost wore, that his throat had been torn open. There was one distinct wound right in the center, and it made Shane think that someone had ripped out the man's throat before he died. He wondered if it had been done by hand or if one of the ghosts had bitten into him and chewed out the missing piece.

"If your friends want to come for a run, I'm all for it, Hugh. Or you can stay and chat, but I need to move," Shane said.

He could already hear the other ghosts approaching, and the incessant sloppy, grinding sound of their movements. The weather would never touch them; the cold would never freeze the dampness. They were eternally rotting, gravid with moisture, squishing and squelching as they moved.

"What does that mean?" Hugh asked of the bloody ghost, ignoring Shane.

"Captain McKenzie has become a part of the island, Mr. Carson. The great horned god claimed him true. He's gone now. Long, long gone."

"He is no god," Hugh said. "Just a man."

The whispering ghosts laughed and jeered. The blood flowed down Wellesley's skull like a faucet had been turned. It rolled over his collar and dripped into the snow at his feet where it pooled, rich and red.

"You know better than that, Mr. Carson. Look at yourself. Look at this world. This is his kingdom, and you have made him angry. You and this man of flesh and fear. He will show you no quarter."

"He is no god," Hugh said again. "You should know better than most. Now that you see what waits for the damned. He is no different from any of us. Just a cursed soul, full of bitterness and hate. You need not fear him.

"Mr. Carson, what fear do you speak of? Do you fear his power? Do you fear his rage?

"We can fight him, Mr. Wellesley. Join us. We will destroy him and bring peace to this island after all these years. Do you not long for peace? Rest?"

Wellesley's bloody jaws parted in a hollow, joyful laugh that was raspy and damp. Blood squirted from the wound in his neck, gushing over his coat and onto the snowy ground.

"Dead men cannot fight gods," the ghost said as though Hugh were a child spouting absurdity.

The rotting spirits had reached the edge of the ridge. Shane reached for Hugh and took him by the arm.

"I'm leaving. Are you?"

The first of the ghosts tumbled down the ridge, rolling like a body being thrown. Shane let Hugh's arm go and began to run again, across the shrub field clearing toward the forest on the other side.

"I will show you the folly of these beliefs," Hugh said a moment after Shane was on his way.

He quickly caught up with Shane, striding easily across the top of the snow. Behind them, the ghosts in the tree called out for him in voices impossible to understand. All but Wellesley, who laughed loudly. The sound grew and grew, echoing among the trees. It started as a mirthful sound, as though the ghost was genuinely amused by what his former crewmate had to say. But it quickly took on the tinge of madness. It was the laughter of someone whose mind was no longer all together.

Shane wondered if all the spirits thought of the King in the same way. Had he somehow convinced them that he was more than just a man? If he had been there for as long as Shane thought, anything was possible. He might have even started to believe that he was a god. Mallory had thought the forest had a spirit, a powerful force that looked out for them. Maybe the island had that idea, and it spread that belief to those who spent too much time there.

Wherever the idea had come from, whoever had started it, and whatever had happened to make the others believe it, Shane was not so easily convinced. To him, the Cannibal King was just a ghost that had grown too big for his britches. He might have long ago forgotten who he was, and he might have become convinced of his power, but anyone who felt that way often just needed a reality check. The kind that came from being beaten, broken, and, in this case, destroyed.

"The King is no god," Hugh said, joining Shane as they entered the tree line beyond the ridge.

"Think I don't know that?" Shane asked.

"Those men would have known that once. I ask that you remember it if he kills you. If he tortures and brings you back as one of those broken creatures, remember that. He is no god. Just an abomination."

Shane failed to suppress a chuckle. Hugh glared at him as grimly as his ruined face could muster.

"This is not a joke," he said.

"No," Shane agreed. "But you're still talking like I'm going to die."

"It stands to reason," Hugh said.

"Call me unreasonable, then," Shane told him.

CHAPTER 14

TO KILL A KING

"In all my years here, I had never seen my crewmates," Hugh said unbidden.

If the forest was still laid out the way it was supposed to be, they were heading north. Directions meant nothing anymore, of course. The island could plunk them right back down in the village at a moment's notice if it wanted to. It was hard to tell if anything Shane saw from one moment to the next was even real.

"Looks like they stay hidden," Shane offered.

"Or they are not permitted to leave," Hugh suggested. "They were good men, once. Most of them. Competent sailors. Decent enough people. Mr. Bundy had spent time in prison for robbery, but he had always been reliable on our ship. He was a good card player. He had a daughter somewhere. Mr. Lowell had a gentle way about him."

"And Red Skull?" Shane asked.

"Mr. Wellesley. Ronald Wellesley. I'd heard he sailed around the world. He survived a bout with the pox. He hunted a lion in Africa. And he rescued a man from a tiger shark in the waters off New Holland. They say he jumped in and fought it with his bare hands."

"Tough guy," Shane said.

Shane was breathing heavily, even though the snow was not as bad this far north. The footing was poor, and sinking into even a few inches of snow made running harder than it needed to be, more tiring, and therefore much more dangerous.

They had lost sight of the subterranean ghosts some time ago, but

Shane did not think this would be like his last encounter in the cabin. Based on Hugh's encounter with his former crewmates, it seemed like the King and the island were aware of what the two were doing. They didn't perceive them as a threat, but they also were not ignoring them.

"He had fortitude, and he was a Christian man, as much as any of us were. We did not attend services regularly, but every sailor prayed when the need arose."

"Death, disaster, and desperation breeds faith," Shane said.

"Yes," Hugh agreed. "But to see him like this, calling this man a god…"

"Not a man," Shane reminded him. "Something dead. Far removed from a man."

Hugh was silent for a moment after that.

"Am I no longer a man?" he asked.

The question was not voiced as a challenge to Shane's statement; it sounded rhetorical. Like Hugh was wondering for the first time, for himself, if there was truth to it.

"Are you?" Shane asked.

Something was lost when a ghost came back. Shane had seen more than one inhuman creature that still bore the face of a man. Some could fit right into a crowd. Some were like Hugh and looked like nightmares. Some looked much worse. But appearances were often deceiving.

Like the living, a ghost was made up of more than what they looked like on the outside. A pretty face could hide an evil heart just as easily as a monstrous face could hide a good one.

Shane wasn't sure what he meant by being a man, though. There were different ways to define what that meant. Shane didn't think there was anything noble in the concept of being a man. A man was just a human. A person like anyone else. They could be good or bad, horrible or caring.

In Shane's experience, that was harder to maintain when someone was dead. He couldn't say for certain that a ghost was human. He thought life had to be part of that definition. A ghost was the leftovers, the bits left behind. And because they were leftovers, parts were missing.

Even the ghosts he lived with were not the people they once had been. Eloise, a nine-year-old girl, could kill with her bare hands. There was no way she had been like that when she was alive.

His companion was not looking for Shane's musings on his existential crisis, and Shane did not want to offer them. The ghost could decide for himself who and what he was.

Hugh slowed to a stop. Shane stopped with him, looking around the forest, and back the way they had come. He needed to take a break soon anyway, to catch his breath. There was still no sign of the other ghosts behind them, not even their sounds carrying on the wind. They had put some significant distance between them, but it would not last.

"I had hoped that if everyone got off the island, there would be no need to worry about the King," Hugh said. "Without any more victims, I had hoped he would just keep to himself. I do not think I can hold on to that hope, Shane. I think he needs to be destroyed. To have this thing free, roaming the land, and convincing others that he is a god, is not natural. It is a second injustice; a second atrocity committed against everyone who is already dead. I do not wish for that to continue."

"Glad we're on the same page now," Shane said.

"I am… afraid." The ghost forced the word out. The reluctance was clear, and he cast his eyes down.

"Of the King?"

"Of dying again," Hugh answered. "I have been this thing for so long that I barely remember anything else. This is not a good existence, but it is mine. It is all I have."

A ghost did not often express fear. Certainly not to Shane. Even those he lived with were not inclined to express feelings like that. Fear was often stripped away in the transition between life and death. After all, there was not much left to lose. It seemed that Hugh had not viewed his existence that way.

"That's why you avoid the King," Shane said.

"Yes. He had no interest in me, and I did not tempt fate. The others did their part well enough. Until you came."

"And turned everything upside-down." Shane nodded.

Hugh's attitude toward Shane made more sense now. He had been confrontational, hostile, apathetic, and disinterested at best in their brief time together. It made more sense in context. Shane represented the end of Hugh's world, the world that he had lived in for more than a hundred years. Maybe two hundred. No matter what kind of existence Hugh had, he was used to it after that much time. Something threatening it would be unwelcome. But Hugh also presumed that Shane would get him destroyed, leaving the King to run amok.

"Well then, it's in both of our interests to destroy him," Shane pointed out.

"It may truly be thus," Hugh agreed.

The ghost looked across the forest ahead of them as though searching for something. Shane looked back the way they had come. He thought he saw movement in the distance, but it was hard to know for sure. Low to the ground, as the ghosts were, they were not easy to see in the dark and through the trees. It could have been a trick of the eye, but he was not willing to gamble on such things. Not on the island.

"I think there is a place near here," Hugh said. "I have not been there in a very long time. But it is formed from the rock like it was forced up through the forest floor. Crags and ridges and one dreadful maw, like a doorway into hell itself."

"A cave?" Shane asked. The ghost was getting a little overdramatic.

"It is not natural. It does not look natural. It does not feel natural. It is where he comes from. Maybe where he died, where his body remains. It is old; that is all I know. And there was a foul air from it like the rotten innards of an old kill."

"So maybe he'd still be there. Bound to his corpse," Shane said.

"I think so. But I do not know how deep the tunnel goes. I do not know what exists beneath our feet."

"Nothing good," Shane replied. "But it only gets worse if we wait."

Shane wanted to keep heading north. He didn't know where the ghosts from underground were bound or where their haunted items existed, but they had been very near the southern tip of the island. They would likely soon reach the edge of their range. That could be an advantage for them, or it could mean that the island would think of a new plan. That it would send something new to get them, like the ghosts from the trees. Shane didn't want to focus on them that much. The sooner they could find the King in his castle, the better.

"This way," Hugh said at last.

His direction seemed arbitrary to Shane's eyes. Neither of them fully recognized the forest they were in, but Shane gave the ghost the benefit of the doubt. He had more experience and more time to recognize landmarks, even subtle and insignificant ones. If there was a cave system, Hugh was the only one between them who knew it existed.

The snow diminished the farther they traveled along the unseen path that existed in Hugh's head. Shane kept pace with the ghost, even though the landscape became more treacherous. Rocks appeared in the soil. There were small ridges and jagged protrusions between trees until the tree cover became sparse. The maples could not root in the rocky soil, and the forest gave way to less hardy shrubs, reduced to little more than tumbleweeds.

Fir trees became more prevalent, their roots more forgiving in the rocky terrain. Some grew right out of the stone. The coverage was still few and far between, giving Shane a little more ability to see where he was going, such as it was. Between the cloud-filled sky and the perpetual night, there was not much to see beyond darkness in every direction.

Hugh stopped abruptly. He put out a hand, its ragged palm against Shane's chest, and stopped him from going forward next to a half-broken granite boulder. Shane said nothing, looking from the ghost's face to where his gaze was directed.

There was nothing to see at first, but the longer Shane concentrated, and the longer Hugh kept his hand on his chest, the more he could make out what he was seeing in the distance. Something moved between the fir trees.

It was shadows hidden in shadows. Shane had to focus more on the perception of movement than on any actual physical forms. They were walking things, not crawling on the ground. He recognized them. Part of him had expected to see them sooner.

"From the trees," Shane said.

"Yes," Hugh replied softly. "I see many."

"How far to the cave?"

"Just past them."

"Are they guarding it?" Shane asked.

"I can't tell yet. But they are not coming for us. They are waiting."

"Well, let's not keep them waiting."

Shane started moving again, pushing Hugh's hand aside and focusing on the place where he thought he had seen something move a short time ago. If the ghosts were protecting the King, the way to get into the earth, or whatever the island was doing, Shane would make them work for it.

CHAPTER 15

WHAT LIES BENEATH

The ghost made a sound like something being dragged through dry leaves. It was raspy and muffled. It came from deep within the desiccated chest as Shane's fist crushed it, shattering the ribs and ancient muscle.

It fell to the ground, now only capable of making a clicking sound, grasping with the one hand that remained attached to its body at the hole Shane had punched through it. Shane said nothing as he stomped on its skull, breaking it with little effort and destroying the spirit before moving on to the next one.

The mummified ghosts in the woods were like the ones he had seen nailed to the trees, but not exactly. These looked like they had been done more lazily. Less effort had been put into torturing them. It looked like they had been killed en masse, just a quick and dirty operation to get them out of the way. Few had been skinned or gutted the way the ones Shane had seen before.

He wondered if these were older or younger than the ones he had fought. They could have been older, made before the King had developed a taste and skill for how he killed his victims. Maybe the ones Shane had seen put on display in the tree were the ones the King was most proud of. The ones who had survived the longest while he did unspeakable things to their bodies. Maybe he was showing them off like trophies.

These other ones lacked the intricacies of the ghosts Shane had fought. They could have been failures; people who died too soon. Or they could have been made before the process was perfected. These curious thoughts ran through Shane's head as he destroyed them, pondering the effort that went into murdering each individual victim, and whether the killer even cared that much about what he did.

The thought process was morbid, but Shane was no stranger to morbid thoughts. It always struck him as unusual when he came across something like what the King was doing on the island. Where the act of killing these people, mutilating them, and putting them on display had become either clinical or recreational; something done with a detached sense of curiosity or disinterest.

Shane wondered at what point someone became completely detached. He had known living men who killed, and they could do so without feeling. He had known snipers with dozens of confirmed kills. He had taken lives himself. But to do what the King was doing on the island was unlike anything he had seen.

It was like someone collecting comic books or coins not for the sake of enjoying them, but for the sake of accumulating the numbers and nothing else. To have the most, the biggest, the best. The most death. The biggest death. The best death.

To kill like that, on that scale, and in the way that the people on the island were killed, meant something. Shane thought it indicated a fundamental failure of humanity. A person—or a ghost—who could do that was horribly broken. That concept was far more terrifying than any of the atrocities he was dealing with in the dark woods.

Hugh was at Shane's side. The ghost attacked the others, removing their heads and destroying them as quickly as he could. Unlike the earlier spirits, these were aware of Hugh and were as willing to fight him as they were to fight Shane. But they were clumsy, slow, and weak. As before, it was more of a nuisance than a proper distraction.

Shane had stopped considering that the plan was to kill him. He thought what he saw now was simply a display of strength. Not the strength of the ghosts, but the strength of the island. It threw numbers at him to show him what it had done. The numbers represented life and time.

Look how many lives were lost. Guess how much time had passed. The death represented generations. And as weak as they were individually, as a group, it was a remarkable display of power. The island was the most prolific serial killer Shane had ever heard of. The King, the island, the two together, however it worked. The bloodlust was undeniable.

Shane circled one of the small fir trees growing from the rocky soil and stopped, nearly running into a faceless ghost that walked toward him with a limp. Something had removed the front of the ghost's skull. There were no eyes, no nose, and no upper jaw. The bone left behind was ragged around the edges. Shane saw the inside of its skull and the shadowy mass of what might have been a brain.

The ghost reached for Shane with fleshless fingers, and he batted aside its hands. They had no power behind them, whatsoever. Stepping up to the ghost, Shane punched into the gap in its head, pushing his hand into a cold, spongy mass, and then continued right through the back. The skull shattered, and for an instant, his arm was straight through the ghost's head.

A weak rush of energy caused Shane to stumble as the ghost burst, vanishing as though it never was. He moved on to the next one, a short spirit missing both eyes but retaining the rest of its features. Shane brought an elbow down hard onto the top of its head, and it collapsed and then exploded.

He kept moving forward, ignoring the ones that were close but not close enough. He didn't need to destroy them; he just needed to get past them. Hugh was also single-minded and moving forward, annoyed that the ghosts were attacking him and forcing him to deal with them. The previous fight had been much easier for him, but this was a hassle.

"Do you see there?" Hugh wrenched the head off a ghost that had been clawing at his legs.

Shane peered into the night. He thought he saw a large grouping of pale, gray stones. There was nothing remarkable from where he stood. They were a good distance away, surrounded by a scattering of the spindly fir trees.

"The rocks?"

"That is where we need to go," Hugh confirmed.

Shane nodded. The distance to the rock was not great, but there were many trees along the way, all shrouded in shadow. He could not say how many ghosts were hidden in the poor light. The journey would be slower than he wanted, but he would not be deterred.

He moved as quickly as he dared over the uneven ground, still slippery with clumps of snow that hid dangers like exposed roots and jagged stones. Many of the ghosts clung to the trees, using them to stay upright as though the act of standing was too much effort. They swung into view from places hidden behind the trunks or deep within the obscuring green needles, and Shane was met with a new monstrosity each time.

When he was close enough to see the rocks more clearly, the density of the ghosts guarding it had thinned out considerably. Only a handful of the spirits were close to where Hugh said their destination awaited. After destroying two of them, Shane realized that no others waited. They were not guarding the cave; they were just blocking the path.

Shane was in a field of stone. He had never seen a natural formation like it. It looked like the rocks had been pushed out from underground, some of them in tall spires, taller than a man, that reached up like teeth from underground.

There were boulders scattered about, rocks larger than cars. Some were cracked, and one was broken open like an egg, but most were covered in a thin, pale layer of lichen.

The stones reminded Shane of crystal formations, the way something like amethyst would form in a geode, but this was simple rock, nothing remarkable, and just jutting out of the earth. He wondered if the island had forced it up, creating the opening and forcing all the stone out of the way so there could be a cave to places below.

Shane imagined that was the case. The island vomiting up its insides to make a home, a prison, a labyrinth inside its guts in which to hold the dead. The house on Berkley Street was not as powerful, but it was not much different from the house rearranging its floor plan, from connecting halls and doors that had no business existing. From creating the ghost of a floor that didn't even exist where the old man and his violin sometimes played.

"You have no idea what's down there?" Shane asked. "How far it goes?"

"I do not," Hugh admitted.

He led them through the spires of stone and Shane followed, looking back to see if any of the dry, shambling ghosts were pursuing them. He saw none.

The giant stone columns looked ominous as he walked around them. Many leaned at steep angles, and the fact that they were still upright seemed impossible. They must have weighed thousands of pounds, and yet they were seemingly completely secure. There was no evidence that any had even broken, even with the shaking of the earth he had just experienced.

Hugh led them through what felt like a maze, around and behind the many stone spires and columns until he came to a stop and Shane joined him.

The ghost had told him that the cave was not natural, but Shane was not sure what Hugh had meant until he saw it. Even though there was no light to speak of, and the sky was black, a glow came from the stone. It was a faint, silvery shine that allowed it to stand out against the impossible darkness of whatever it concealed.

It was not a cave like Shane had expected. This was something new. This was a chasm. The entrance was ten yards across and more than that high, with long, thin spires of stone hanging from the top, like the jaws of a vampire.

The air coming from the cave was warmer than the ambient air outside. It was also damp enough to produce steam that rose in thin wisps.

It carried a stench with it, something Shane couldn't put his finger on. It smelled like dead things but something more. Like rotting vegetables, stagnant water, and things that had been forgotten in the dark for too long. There was a sweet undertone to it like the smell of molasses, that made it even more revolting.

"Are you ready?" Hugh asked.

Before Shane could answer, the steam coming from the cave swirled, twisting and spiraling as a gust of warm air belched out. It carried a deep, resonant moan with it. Like the sounds he heard when the wind blew around the island, only focused now and coming from a single exit like a monstrous horn being blown.

The sound grew louder and louder, and then it took on a rhythm. It pulsed a repetitive, droning sound, coming from everywhere under Shane's feet. It was emerging from the cave, but the island was summoning it from all corners. The thrumming grew louder, vibrating, until Shane felt it in his legs. The boom-boom-booming sound continued slow and steady, and he realized after a moment what he was hearing.

It was a pulse. A heartbeat.

CHAPTER 16
UNTO THE BREACH

Frank approached the island at a slow, steady pace. The sea was choppy, and the white caps heading onto the island's shore revealed, and then hid, the rocky protrusions around the inlet leading to the dock. The boat he piloted had a shallow draft and was unlikely to run afoul of many of them even if he went right over the top, but he didn't want to risk it. If the island wanted to destroy him, it would do so easily enough, and he didn't need to give it a hand.

He had no idea where to look for Shane. He had no idea if he was even prepared to look for him. Frank had picked up some more iron items in the mainland before he left: an iron bar and some loose iron filings from a local metal shop that he had scooped into bags and put in his pocket.

He had also brought a flashlight, matches, and extra food and water. Just basic survival gear. They might not have been much help, but they would allow him to escape and survive in a pinch if he got into a tough situation. Without Shane around, he could only do so much on his own, and he had no idea what was left on the island.

It had seemed like only the King was left, and Hugh, but whatever the Shane thing was, Frank doubted it was alone. Illusion or ghost, there was power on the island, and it was dangerous. He wanted to be as prepared as he could be.

Snow was falling on the island. The storm extended only a short distance around the rock. It was not intense, certainly not a blizzard, but it fell at a good pace. It looked unnatural from a distance like the island had been singled out while the rest of the ocean remained untouched.

Frank had a sense of foreboding in his stomach. It was his fight-or-flight response telling him that fighting was stupid, and running was the only sensible option.

Frank had been frightened many times in his life. He had seen things most people would never believe. He had felt cold terror set right into his bones. But the feeling that he got when he looked at the island was something unusual even for him. He wondered if that, too, was part of the island's illusion. Was it making him feel like he didn't need to come back? Like he was a fool to try?

The island clearly wanted him to leave. Something had literally escorted him away from it. It didn't want him back, but it was also not stopping him. The seas remained navigable and calm. No rogue waves appeared to dash his boat on the rocks. He didn't understand what was happening. Or why.

The inlet drew closer, and the snow began to fall on the deck of Frank's boat. A thought occurred to him as he puzzled out why the island helped him escape but did nothing to prevent his return other than mounting a sense of impending dread. He thought of it like he would think of any ghosts. He was giving it human motivation.

If the island was responsible for much of what they were experiencing, he could not anthropomorphize it. It was not a man; it had never been a man. It was spirit energy that might have come from dead men, but it was not conscious. It could not think like that. What he was dealing with had to be more instinct and emotion. There couldn't be rationality, sense, or consciousness. It was little more than an animal, if that.

It was only a thought, but it made sense to Frank. He couldn't think of the island like any other ghost. It couldn't work the same way. If that was the case, he wasn't sure he could ever understand it. It was hard enough to get into someone else's head. How could he get into the head of something that didn't have a head to begin with?

Frank took his small boat through the inlet to the wooden dock near the shore. He heard the wind howling through the hidden caverns beneath the island in a low, moaning sound from the woods. The island was acknowledging his presence, greeting him upon his return. Not necessarily a warm welcome, but a welcome, nonetheless.

He tied the boat off with a rope around one of the support posts buried deep under the water. He then made his way down the wooden slats toward the small landing that served as a beach just before the western cliff face of the island. The zigzagging path was empty save for snow. Nothing moved in the shadows, and nothing crept from the sea.

The last place Frank had seen Shane for certain was on the other side of the island. They were in the southeast when Frank had left him. He would have to journey past the village toward emptiness. There was nothing out there, no landmarks or anything that looked even remotely memorable. And with the snowfall, there was no way Shane had left tracks. But Frank had to try.

The trip up the zigzag path was slow. The snow made it slick, and he nearly slipped more than once. There were no handholds along the way, only the rock on the wall itself, which he put a hand on to steady himself as best he could. The wind occasionally kicked up sudden gusts that swept at him from behind and threatened to push him forward. Frank no longer trusted anything on the island to be natural, but the gusts were not violent enough to knock him over. They threatened and teased dangerously, but not seriously. Not yet.

Frank reached the top, and the island looked just as he expected it to. A field of white was laid out before him. He saw the maple forest in the distance to the left. To his right, he knew there was a path, small and indistinct beneath the snow, that led to the village.

There was no smoke in the air, and no signs of life now that everyone was gone but Shane. If he had made his way back to the village, he would have started a fire. It would have been the smart thing to do. But Frank saw nothing. The storm was not so bad that it would conceal signs of smoke from a chimney.

Frank made his way through the snow. It wasn't as deep as it had been, just barely to the top of his boots. He didn't remember the exact path, but he knew the direction well enough. His progress was not so bad, and when he finally came upon the village, standing high at the edge of the hill that surrounded it, there was nothing to see when he looked down but the empty, snow-covered cabins.

There was no smoke, no sign of tracks, and no evidence that anyone had opened a door or a window since they left. The village was abandoned. Or so it seemed. He wasn't willing to write Shane off just yet.

Frank walked and half-slid down the snow-covered edge of the bowl around the village, and then navigated through the irregular maze of shacks. Each one was empty, with no sign that anything had happened since he'd left with the others. Shane wasn't there, and it didn't look like he had been.

The snow continued to fall. There was no noise apart from the distant sound of the waves. Frank saw nothing moving, and no signs of life or death. He worked south, climbing over the shallow edge of the bowl and back up into the field of white.

It was a more arduous journey on this side of the island. The snow was deeper, for some reason. The wind angled more toward him, freezing his eyebrows and cheeks as he went. Frank spent much of his time with his face down, only lifting his head occasionally to make sure he was on track. Even then, it was hard. He didn't know what he was moving toward, and he didn't know where to look for Shane. When Frank had left him, there was nothing around but snow, the cliff edge, and the ocean beyond.

The fake Shane had said he found a way down, the same way Brandon had told them about before he'd disappeared. Maybe the real Shane had done the same. If anyone would find the path, it would be Shane. Frank just needed to retrace his friend's steps, a job easier said than done with the snow concealing everything.

Frank angled to the east at the southern tip of the island and followed along the rocky ledge. He looked over when it was safe to, making sure to brace himself against any sudden gusts of wind that might kick up to send him to his death. He would not underestimate the island again. He would be as prepared as he could, but he would still not give up until he discovered Shane's fate.

Frank walked farther than he felt he should have. He could no longer consider himself at the southern tip of the island. Now, he was walking up the eastern wall. Nothing looked even remotely different. No sign of a path, and no sign of the hidden cove Brandon had told them about. Definitely no sign of Shane.

Frank's frustration mounted. He was tired of chasing his tail. The people of the village had been saved. He didn't want to engage in games anymore. He wanted to be done with the place.

"If you want us gone, then let us go," he said out loud. "Show me where to go. Show me how to end this and leave you in peace."

It was a hopeless thing to say. Foolish, even. Frank couldn't acknowledge that he thought the island didn't have intelligence or intellect like a man and then ask it for favors in the same breath. Nor would he expect it to grant a favor, no matter what kind of sentience the place had. It had proven untrustworthy enough times already. It, or the Cannibal King. Both wanted death. Frank put no faith in either of them.

At the same time, Frank acknowledged that he wasn't necessarily speaking to the island. His faith was not bound to a haunted place. And when he asked for clarity, when he asked to be shown the way, he was not asking evil things. Even if they were listening.

He continued along the eastern wall, angling north until he decided he had gone too far. The ocean below crashed against the rocks again and again, the constant rush of water the only sound that reached his ears. Frank turned and headed back the way he had come. He hoped the new angle might give him a different perspective, allow him to see something ahead that he'd missed in the other direction.

A gust of wind came right up the wall, blasting Frank vertically and forcing him to stumble. He lost his footing on a slick, icy rock and fell. Rolling quickly and holding onto whatever he could reach to steady himself, he scrambled to keep from falling off the edge.

Frank lay there for a long moment, face-down in the snow, breathing heavily. In an instant, he had almost died. No ghost, no epic battle, just a slippery rock.

He lifted his head and looked to the left. A nearly perfect line of snow ran down the side of the cliff. The snow was sitting atop something that, without it, he would not have seen otherwise. A ledge was there. A path down.

Frank stayed on his knees, his eyes locked on the snowy ledge, and crawled toward it. It was almost impossible to see the path until he was right on top of it, but it was wide enough for a man to descend before it wrapped around the wall to parts unseen.

"Thank you," Frank said quickly, glancing skyward.

He made his way cautiously down the path.

Chapter 17
Entombed

Frank stared down at the small cove nestled against the island's edge. It was almost a perfect little lagoon and would have been an ideal place to store the boats in an emergency. Brandon had been right.

The snowy path down the wall had curved along the side high above the cove and continued toward a cavern entrance in the island's eastern face. The fake Shane had told the truth, limited though it was, about what he'd discovered. Frank thought Shane must have come this way for real. Whether he was still there was another matter.

Frank headed to the cave entrance to see what was inside. Even with the flashlight from his bag, there was little to see. The shape of the rock prevented much snow from accumulating, acting as a natural shield. Inside, a tunnel extended around a bend and left no clues as to what remained. There was damp stone and no more. Frank stepped inside.

The distant sound of the howling wind came to his ears within moments of entering the cave. The tunnels must have all connected somewhere. It gave the effect of something far off moaning like a horrible, sad thing that was tired and in pain.

A short distance into the cave, he found a body slumped down against the wall where the person had died. From the looks of the corpse—barely more than bones with some mummified flesh attached—it had been long ago.

There was nothing remarkable about the body. Frank saw no ghost attached, and there was nothing on the dead man's person that offered insight into what had killed him, or when. There was also no sign of Shane.

The only thing Frank noticed that was even slightly out of place was the odor. Not the skeletal remains of the man in the tunnel, but something deeper in the underground. It smelled like burnt oil, as if someone had recently set something on fire.

Frank continued deeper into the tunnel, careful with his footing on the wet stone, looking for any signs of life, branching paths, or anything to indicate Shane might have been down there.

Eventually, he discovered the remains of a broken lantern. There was still a small bit of oil on the ground, and it looked as though it had been burned recently. Frank touched it, and it was ice cold. Still, given the time frame, it could have been Shane. It was definitely more recent than the dead man on the ground.

The tunnel took a left turn not far from the smashed oil lantern and opened into a large cavern. Frank swept the beam of the flashlight across the space. It was so large that it could have served as an auditorium.

He directed the yellow beam of light to the cavern floor. His muscles tensed, and he froze for a moment, the beam vibrating slightly. He scanned the cavern floor slowly from left to right. He realized he had been holding his breath and let it out in a soft, controlled exhale.

The cavern floor was invisible, obscured from view under the scattered, skeletal remains of hundreds of bodies. Frank had never seen so many corpses in one place. It was like a failed ossuary, bones piled upon bones from one side of the room to the other.

There was no rhyme or reason to the spread of the bodies. It looked as though they had been left wherever they had fallen. There were unusual clusters in some spots; a pile of skulls in one place, a half-dozen rib cages almost on top of each other in another. Maybe something had moved them at some point. Maybe they had all been killed together in one go.

There were scraps of clothing, but much of it was rotted away. Time and the damp conditions of the cave had taken their toll. It was hard for Frank to tell how old any of them might have been, if they had come from the same time, or had built up over the years. They all looked the same—just dirty, fleshless bones.

He counted them for a while. It was a habit of his when confronted by a large group of anything. In the back of his mind, he would start rattling off the numbers to get a sense of what he was dealing with. But there was no way to account for everything he saw. His count reached one hundred skulls before he barely left the farthest corner of the cavern. He guessed four hundred dead, maybe five hundred, maybe even more.

"My God," Frank whispered.

So many people, all lost together in the dark. What wretched fate must they all have met? What horrible thing the island, or its denizens, must have done to them all?

It couldn't have happened at the same time. Frank couldn't even imagine this many people being on the island together at one time. What he was looking at must have been the product of years of work. Years of death.

This was not the cannibals, not the ghosts that he and Shane had fought. Maybe the Cannibal King. Maybe the island itself. But something had worked, putting in time and dedication to kill everyone who came to Maple Grove.

Frank had no doubt that the island was old. The killing was old. Death had made a home on the island for a very long time. Much longer than Hugh Carson had been there.

As he searched the mass grave with his light, Frank caught sight of something dark on the far side of the cavern. Another cave was there, a tunnel that continued deeper into the island. Since there were no signs of Shane, and there had been no other branching paths, it was his only option.

Shane would have been less startled by the sight of so many bodies. He wouldn't have let it sway him. He wouldn't have turned and gone back the way he came. He would have pressed on, looking for the Cannibal

King and a way to end everything. And that meant Frank would do the same.

Frank stepped fully into the cavern. The bodies were in a recessed section, almost like a sunken floor. It was impossible to find clear space without bones in the way, so Frank was forced to move bodies, kicking them aside to find solid ground beneath them.

The act felt disrespectful. He didn't want to kick the dead out of his way, but there was no graceful way to do it. There was no way to treat all those people with the dignity they deserved. Someone would have to come back for them at some point. Except, he knew, that would never happen. They could not send anyone back to the island.

Frank stood there, up to his ankles in the damp remains of hundreds of unknown souls. He could offer little comfort to any of them. There were no ghosts there, no one to hear his words. But their souls still deserved something.

"Eternal rest grant unto them, O Lord," Frank said softly. He did not have the words for a stronger prayer. He wasn't sure there was one. "Let perpetual light shine upon them. May they rest in peace. Amen."

Frank began moving cautiously through the cavern. He extended his leg and used the tip of his boot to ease whatever bones were in the way aside until he had a clear spot in which to step. It made his progress agonizingly slow, but he had no interest in crushing bones beneath his feet, or further disrespecting those who had met their end there.

Step by step, Frank made his way across the cavern. In the distance, he heard the wind moaning in the tunnels. The sounds he and Shane had heard in the woods, like the mournful cries of some kind of monster, were very different beneath the ground. It sounded so much bigger and more powerful, echoing through the stone. It was like he was creeping toward a sleeping giant's lair.

Bones rattled as they tumbled out of the way, some of them too precarious for him to step past nimbly or gently. He winced every time, cringing at the implication of disturbing the dead and casting new indignities upon them. But there was nothing to be done for it. As much as he needed to respect the dead, the living required the most attention. He needed to find Shane. He needed to get them both off the island and put the place behind them.

By the time Frank reached the tunnel at the far end of the cavern, he had made his way past so many bodies that he realized it would have been impossible to count them all. They were stacked several deep in some places. The dead had been tossed upon the dead. The cavern was not a place where they died, it was just where they were dumped, maybe to keep them out of sight of new victims.

It made Frank wonder about the rage of whoever was responsible. The King. That had to be the only answer. What sort of man was he when he was alive? What sort of person becomes such a monster after they die?

Frank had met his share of killer spirits. Not as many as Shane, but he knew them. He had tried to understand them. He had negotiated with some to find out if there was a way to get past what they had become and embrace their humanity again. Sometimes, it worked. Sometimes, it was just a matter of dealing with the horrible anger they felt and bringing them back to something calmer and more manageable.

There were times, however, when there was no way to deal with a ghost. Frank did not even need to meet the Cannibal King face to face to know he would be one of those. He was not a ghost they would talk to or negotiate with. He was no longer the ghost of a man, he was just the ghost of anger. The ghost of hunger. He was a thing that had no remorse. But he did have cruelty, and that made him especially dangerous.

Frank entered the new tunnel. There were no bodies here, no signs of lanterns or burnt oil. It was the only direction Shane could have gone, though. If he was still below, Frank would find him.

The wind howled again as he made his way deeper into the island. The noise was closer now, but at the same time, some parts sounded so far away. It had become almost like a harmony. Frank wasn't certain if that made it more or less unsettling.

The air grew warmer the deeper he traveled. The chill of the outside could not penetrate so deep, but the moisture increased. The tunnel smelled of age, of things gone rotten in the dampness and the dark. But it betrayed no secrets. No tracks, no signs of life. All he could do was follow the path laid out before him.

Where are you, Shane? Frank thought.

His only answer was the deep, miserable moan of the wind through the caves.

CHAPTER 18
THE MOUTH OF HELL

The steam rolled across Shane's face, and it felt like a wet blanket being dragged over his flesh. The smell was fishy and sour like fermented guts. He felt his stomach turning but forced it from his mind. He would not be overcome with a cheap trick so easily.

Hugh smelled nothing and made his way into the cave, unaware but still hesitant. It was not the smell or the temperature that gave the ghost pause. It was centuries of conditioning, of fear that this was where death—true death—waited.

The beat continued, thumping like a massive heart in the center of the earth. When Shane had solid rock beneath his feet, he felt it up through his legs and into his gut. He stood still, humidity soaking into his clothes in stark contrast to the freezing temperatures only a few feet behind him, and breathed slowly.

"What are you doing?" Hugh's voice tinged with urgency.

"It's my heartbeat," he said.

The ghost was perplexed. Shane stayed where he was, feeling his heartbeat in his chest and hearing it in his ears as the blood rushed through his veins. The island had synchronized itself with him. The powerful *thump-thump* matched perfectly with his pulse. It was almost overwhelming, and he had to shake his head to clear his mind and tear his focus away.

"It's only a trick," Hugh offered.

"I know," Shane said. "A good one, though."

"I wouldn't know. We should get moving. I do not like being exposed here."

"Yeah," Shane said.

He looked back the way they had come. There were no ghosts approaching. None came anywhere near the cave or the stony protrusions from the ground. Either they were not allowed, or they knew better.

Shane headed deeper into the cave with Hugh at his side. Even though the air was moist, rancid, and bordering on hot as whatever gas from below billowed up with the thrumming of Shane's heartbeat, the cave floor was strangely dry.

The path they were meant to follow narrowed considerably after the wide entrance. The mouth part of the cave, laced with stone fangs, was like a foyer, a grand entrance to welcome him and Hugh into what was coming. But the tunnel was less ostentatious, dry, and empty of everything but the smell and the sound.

There was little on the floor, not even loose stones. The rock was smooth, even like it had been made that way on purpose. Shane wondered if that were true. The look of everything was very intentional. The island could have birthed the entire thing, forced up the stone, forged it into the shape of a mouth, and refined all the details to make it look the way it did. Just another intimidation play, another gimmick.

If the entrance was a mouth, and the metaphor continued, the tunnel was the throat. It led down into the earth, into the guts below. Into whatever was very aware that Shane and Hugh were coming.

Shane was not foolish enough to think that fighting the King would be easy. He hoped Hugh had the motivation to do what needed to be done if the situation got out of hand.

Shane did not intend to waste time. The island had already wasted enough. Frank was out there somewhere, and so were the villagers. Shane had allowed the King to flex his strength for too long. He'd let the ghost get too cocky. It sounded like he had spent hundreds of years existing that way, being the big dog. Shane was ready to put him in his place. To put him down.

The rhythm of the pulse did not subside. The boom from deep in the ground vibrated through the rock. As Shane and Hugh continued down the tunnel into the darkness below, new sounds joined it.

It was already dark when they entered the mouth-like cave, but Shane was thrown off by what came next. The tunnel was pure black; the deepest sort of darkness Shane had ever experienced. He had to move slowly and carefully, using his other senses to guide him. His sense of touch was the most useful, as the sound in the cave soon became a distraction.

Though faint at first, Shane realized he was listening to voices. Not whispers, just distant conversation. He could not make out what was being said, only that there was more than one speaker, and they sounded pitched, fervent, energetic, and maybe even anxious.

"You need to move faster," Hugh said after just a few minutes of travel.

Shane had his hands on the wall as a guide and support. The floor was moist, slick, and unpredictable. He did not want to use his lighter, didn't want to sacrifice a hand to hold it. Not in that place. He suspected that the island would not have allowed it, anyway. The gusts of stagnant, hot air would have snuffed it, or the gases would prove to be flammable. It was just a hunch, but he felt that the darkness was part of the illusion, and he didn't want to waste energy on something so unimportant.

Before Shane answered, the image of Hugh flared to life before him. He produced a soft, blue-white glow that illuminated him and the tunnel around them. It was not intense, but it was enough for Shane to see where he was walking and gain more secure and confident footing.

"You could have done that sooner," Shane pointed out.

"You weren't this slow until now," Hugh replied.

The voices grew louder, almost in direct response to the appearance of the light. No one was around, no one touched by the faint glow. The tunnel had yet to branch anywhere, and Shane saw no alcoves or hidden places for anyone or anything. But it sounded like they still had a ways to go. There would be time to discover more of the island's secrets.

Even though it was still hard to make out what the voices said, a word sometimes hit Shane's ear with stunning clarity.

"Bones," one said.

"Drag them," another added.

He had played the game before. Whispered threats and ominous tones. The island was becoming a little predictable. It was relying on clichés now. If Shane heard a random scream or chains rattling, he might start laughing.

Hugh led the way with Shane two paces behind, at the edge of the light the ghost cast. In time, the voices shifted, and Shane now heard them from behind, too. He looked back at one point and saw the faintest glimmer of movement, a flash of something vaguely metallic, reflecting Hugh's light. It was far from them, though, many yards back the way they had come, and it lasted only for an instant.

Shane would not be fooled. Anything behind them now had always been behind them. It was likely the same as whatever was in front of them. He was not convinced they were ghosts, just illusions cast by the island. Things conjured up in the subconscious of something that had no business having a mind of its own. Things that preyed on primal fears, which would have worked on most people.

"Fork," Hugh said suddenly.

He stopped at a crossroads. The tunnel split, with the second branch heading to their left and the one they were on continuing straight with a slight decline. The voices Shane heard seemed to come from both directions. Neither looked more appealing than the other, but he nodded to the path they were already on.

"This one goes deeper. Think that's what we need," he said.

"If we're wrong?" Hugh asked.

"Don't think the island would let us make the wrong choice," Shane answered.

The island would not be putting on such a grand production if the intent was just to send them down the wrong path. It was possible that the island would play with them, and make them get lost in the tunnels. Shane could see that being something the King would find amusing.

Back home in Nashua, when his house had been under the influence of the girl in the pond, it had done something similar to Eloise when she was still alive. The little girl had become lost in the spaces between the walls, and the house had not allowed her to find a way out. She heard people outside—her mother and others looking for her—but she could not get to them. She stayed in the walls until she died, a slow and miserable death from hunger and dehydration.

Shane was mostly certain that the house was responding to the cruelty of the girl called Vivienne. There was a symbiotic relationship there, a transfer of feeling. It would not surprise him to see the island working that way with the King. It put him on edge because it made things unpredictable.

When the house moved, trapping Eloise in a wall, or directing someone to a fourth floor that didn't normally exist, those were not illusions. Those were real changes in the physical world. Just like the cave and the tunnel that Shane was in had to be real. But it didn't mean they were natural.

Shane had learned that ghosts were often predictable. Every ghost followed a few rules no matter who they were. Friend or foe, they were banished by iron and able to be trapped in lead or salt. And if they were destroyed, their haunted item was destroyed with them. Knowing that the basics applied to all of them made them easier to deal with.

A haunted place did not follow those rules. Shane didn't know if there were rules for his house, for the island, or anything else that might have been similar out in the world. A fight without rules was a fight he could lose if he wasn't careful. That's why he kept his eyes open. He needed to be ready for anything.

It was a relief that the island was being predictable for now, but that didn't mean it would stay that way. It could have some extra tricks that Shane had never encountered, and that could be a problem. He didn't like heading into unknown situations, even though he was already deep in the bowels of a tunnel that thrummed with the beat of his heart.

As they proceeded down Shane's chosen path, the makeup of the tunnel changed. The color of the stone, even the texture, was different. It seemed rougher now, and there were visible striations like flakes where it had broken off. At some points, they passed indentations in the walls, little segments the size of closets, or even small rooms.

When Shane looked directly at the depressions in the stone, the small rooms, or the stunted passages, there was never anything to see. But if he was not looking, if his focus was ahead, he caught movement out of the corner of his eyes. It was always fleeting, but things were there. Shapes like men, some of them chewed apart like Hugh and the others. Some of them were dried husks, half-dissected like those in the trees.

The shapes were gone whenever Shane looked again. The ghosts, the illusions—whatever they were—were just meant to be on the outskirts of their journey. They were just one more reminder that he was not sneaking up on anything. The King was expecting him. The island was showing him the way. Whatever happened, he needed to be prepared for it. Because it was prepared for him.

"Shane." Hugh came to a stop again.

The tunnel widened ahead of them, and the faint light provided by the ghost showed a series of tunnels that branched away, a honeycomb of paths heading in all directions. In the center of it were spirits, many of them, their eyes all turned to Shane and Hugh.

"Guess the teasing is over," Shane said.

Why not? Haven't had a fight in twenty minutes or so, he thought.

CHAPTER 19

DWELLERS IN THE DEEP

The ghosts in the chamber backed away as the light from Hugh neared them. There was an urgency to their movement, almost a fear, as if they thought the light might hurt them.

These ghosts were not like the other ones that Shane had seen. These ones were much older, and many still wore the clothing of their era. One of them wore the uniform of a colonial marine. Another wore a red coat from the Revolutionary War. Some just wore simple garb that might have belonged to a farmer or a tradesman. Others wore uniforms he recognized as French, British, or Dutch from various time periods, dating back three hundred years or more.

They whispered as Shane and Hugh approached, though no one's lips moved. Whether it was the ghost he was seeing, or ones hidden in shadow, it didn't matter. All eyes were on them. Everyone knew they were there now.

Shane saw that Hugh was tense and ready to fight. The ghost had crouched low, taking up the curious frog pose he always took, with his meatless legs bent and his hands balled into fists. He swayed almost hypnotically, looking from one spirit to the next as though deciding which one to attack first.

The spirits were not aggressive, and they were not attacking, but they did not look friendly, either. Many had been brutally savaged before death. Those that still had faces were scowling, sneering, or otherwise expressing hostility. Nevertheless, none made a move.

Shane was reminded of predators in the wild. Like hyenas when confronted by lions. They were smart enough to back off. They knew not to fight when it was not the right time or place. But the ghosts far outnumbered Hugh and Shane. A dozen were in the chamber, with maybe more hidden beyond the reach of Hugh's light. He did not think fear of losing against Shane and Hugh kept them at bay. It had to be fear of something else.

The King would be no stranger to fighting other spirits. He had been kept underground for years by the cannibals in the forest until Shane thinned their numbers. Maybe these spirits were ones the King had spared and as a result, they feared stepping on his toes. Maybe they had simply been told not to interfere.

Shane stood at the entrance to the chamber, a short distance from Hugh, with his back to a wall. His hands were in fists, and he watched the movement of every ghost as it backed away, staying just at the edge of the light.

"Will you not attack?" Hugh's voice had a sour note to it as though he found their reluctance offensive.

The ghosts did not reply, but the voices continued murmuring in the dark, saying things Shane could not quite make out. They were agitated. They spoke quickly, but the words ran together. Too many voices spoke at the same time. It was hard to make out any of it. The only thing he could tell for certain was that they were angry, and the anger seemed to be directed at him.

"Keep moving," he told Hugh.

"And if they attack?"

"Then they'll regret it."

The ghost of the Redcoat stepped back into the light the moment Hugh got to his feet. Shane had not even started moving, but he turned to face the spirit only a few feet away.

He had been young when he died, in his early twenties, Shane guessed. His hair was dark and shaggy, and his nose had been shifted around from an errant punch or two over the years. He had been a scrapper in life, and his expression in death reflected it.

The ghost's throat had been torn out. It was a brutal wound, and not just to the surface flesh and muscle. Whatever had done it had torn him from below his chin to his collarbone and exposed the spine. The trachea, muscles, and esophagus were all removed. There was very little holding his head up, but as a ghost, that didn't matter.

Aside from the neck wound, the ghost did not appear badly injured. His face was puffy, as though some sickness had taken hold of him, but he looked normal otherwise. His eyes, though bloodshot, still had a keenness, a glimmer that suggested understanding and intention. He was not a mindless thing like the ones from the trees or from the cave on the southern end of the island.

"Something you need, Cromwell?" Shane asked.

He knew the ghost would not answer him. There was nothing he could say even if he wanted to. Not with the condition of his throat. But he bared his teeth, grimacing at Shane as though he might lunge and bite. Shane smiled back.

The colonial Marine at the Redcoat's side stepped forward. Shane chuckled at the contrast between the men. They might have killed each other during the war, but it seemed that the island had brought them together in their hatred.

"Getting bold, I see," Shane said.

From their initial reaction, he expected them to back off and keep their distance. Maybe whatever hold the island, or the King, had on them was limited. Maybe the prospect of a fresh kill right in their faces was more temptation than they could resist.

The Marine had met a more violent end than his British companion. The entire front of his uniform had been torn away, shredded as though by a small blade. The flesh beneath looked as though his body had been slashed open hundreds of times.

The wounds were small but plentiful. They extended from his face to his knees, with barely an inch of skin left untouched. The lower half of his face had gotten the worst of it. From his cheekbones down, it looked like whoever had attacked him had carved away all the skin and muscle, but not with the flat of a blade, just with the tip slicing in again and again. It had made ribbons out of him.

Though he had very little that resembled a mouth left on his face, the remaining, ragged muscle pulled back as the Marine scowled as well, and a bifurcated tongue slipped out to lick his own bloody chin.

The two of them stepping forward had emboldened the others. Those that had shrunk into the shadows scuttled closer, encroaching on the edge of Hugh's light. They were a motley crew of faces, injuries, and time periods. Some looked like they might have been on the island since the fifties, while one of the oldest Shane saw must have come across with the Spanish some five hundred years ago, based on his outfit.

"I do not think they fear you as much as you suspected they did," Hugh offered.

He was still waiting to make a move or for someone else to do so. The muttering had grown as loud as the beating heart sound that vibrated the walls. Whispers, hisses, and muffled curses came from all directions.

Shane didn't answer. They were wasting time. The ghosts were not attacking; they were just trying to intimidate. They were squaring off and, in doing so, slowing him down. He didn't have time for it. Frank could have been down there somewhere, and if he was still alive, Shane wanted to find him. Even if Frank was dead, Shane had no intention of leaving his friend behind. He certainly would not let a room full of grim-faced ghosts stop him.

Rather than waiting for them to make their move, Shane stepped to the Redcoat, stepping on the ghost's foot with his boot while pushing against him with his shoulder at the same time.

The ghost began to fall back and Shane reached out quickly, his hand closing around the exposed spine in the spirit's neck. He kept his foot on the ghost's foot and pulled back in a sharp, jerking motion. The ghost's spine broke in his hand, with segments of spectral bone falling away as he removed the head from the long-dead man's shoulders.

When the ghost's body came apart, the release of energy was far more explosive than the ghosts Shane had recently destroyed. The blast knocked him backward into Hugh, preventing what would have been a much more painful fall. The Marine and the other ghosts around were thrown against the cavern walls as though a grenade had gone off in the center of the room.

Hugh pushed Shane off and got to his haunches before anyone else. He moved even as Shane was getting to his feet, jumping on the Marine. The soldier was not expecting an attack so quickly, and not from another spirit. His defense fell flat, raising his arms as though getting ready to box while Hugh went low and took out his legs.

The Marine growled as he hit the ground. Shane spared the two little attention. He was back on his feet, ready to defend, as the burly ghost of a man dressed in rags came at him from the other side.

Shane could not get ahold of the new ghost as easily as he had the Redcoat. Now that they knew what he was capable of, they were wary. His newest opponent fought defensively, angling Shane away from the wall and toward the other ghosts.

"Not gonna happen, big boy," Shane said as the ghost took a swipe at him designed to make him dodge. Instead, he caught the spirit's wrist and fell back in the opposite direction, putting his weight on the elbow and breaking the arm with a pop.

The ghost cursed in Dutch as he fell to the ground with Shane, his arm hanging uselessly at his side. When he hit the ground, Shane planted an elbow firmly in the spirit's ribs, cracking two with the effort.

Shane was on his feet quickly, but the ghost struggled, not used to permanent injuries. He tried to get up using his broken arm and fell face-first into the rock. Shane's boot came down in a decisive blow on the back of the fallen spirit's head. The resistance was negligible as ghostly flesh crumbled and burst.

The blast was powerful, but Shane caught himself this time, bracing himself against the nearest wall before he fell. Hugh, on the other hand, took advantage of the sudden disruption. He used the force of the blast and rode it toward the wall, twisting the neck of the Marine as he did so. The other spirit gurgled a protest that was cut off violently and wetly as his head pulled from his shoulders.

With three of their number gone, the remaining ghosts were less enthusiastic about continuing the fight. Shane saw in their eyes that they still wanted blood. They were angry, but they were also afraid.

"Only three of you have any balls? King must have taken the rest, huh?" Shane said.

Hugh glared at him, unimpressed, but Shane ignored him, focusing on the ghosts.

"Who's next?"

"Is this how you always fight?" Hugh asked.

Shane grinned, watching the ghosts shuffle in the shadows. He saw the wheels turning, and the decisions being made. They were wondering how to pull it off.

"This is how I fight sad-sack cowards," he said, looking at a ghost with a gaping chest wound in the eye. The ghost was sneering and then looking around at those around him to draw their attention.

"You're thinking you can take me if your buddies help, aren't you?" Shane asked. He smiled broadly, letting it settle into a confident smirk. "You think I won't break his leg first thing?"

He nodded to a shorter ghost, a man in a French sailor uniform from the nineteenth century.

"Then break off your arm before breaking his nose?" Shane targeted the sneering ghost and then the one on his right who could very well have been a farmer from the turn of the century.

None of the ghosts made a move. The Frenchman's expression became unsure.

"Who's next?" Shane asked again.

Part of it was meant to intimidate. They were already nervous after seeing what he and Hugh could do. Part of it was his impatience and anger getting the best of him. He'd had enough of the island and its spirits. He was more than willing to destroy every one of them if that was what they wanted. But he could tell none of them truly wanted it. If any of them had their heart in the game, they would have already attacked. They were looking for an excuse not to do it.

"Let's go," he said to Hugh, heading toward the nearest path out of the chamber. The other ghost was slow to make a move, watching the other hostile spirits from his crouched fighting stance.

"The rest of you can piss off. If I see you again, you won't have the chance to leave," Shane said.

The ghosts were silent as he left. Hugh came after him a moment later, cautious but not wanting to stay behind.

Nothing followed them down the tunnel.

CHAPTER 20
A HISTORY OF VIOLENCE

The pulse continued as Shane and Hugh traveled deeper into the island. The pace had increased slightly until it no longer matched Shane's heartbeat. For a few moments, he thought his heart was racing, but he stopped long enough to realize the island had picked up the tempo on its own.

Whispers continued through the tunnels. From behind, from in front, and sometimes through the narrowest cracks in the stone.

They saw no more ghosts as they walked, but the chill in the air and the voices were convincing reminders that the spirits were not far away. Shane didn't know if they were being followed through the rocks in the shadows. The ones they had left behind were probably still after them, and more besides. Fear had kept them away for a while, but Shane knew the tide could turn at any moment. If anything happened that made the ghosts think they could capitalize and turn the tables on him, he had no doubt they would take advantage.

If the ghosts attacked again, it would not be one at a time. They would swarm to make it impossible to fight them all off. They had learned what Shane could do, and if they were smart, they would do everything they could to avoid it and take him out as quickly as they could.

"Did you recognize all those uniforms?" Shane asked as they walked through the winding tunnel.

"Some," Hugh said, "but not all."

"There was at least one Spaniard in there. A sailor."

"What does that mean?" Hugh asked.

"Esteban Gómez reached the coast of Maine in about 1525. That man's clothes fit the period. There have been dead men here for half a millennium, maybe longer. Some were naked and torn apart. Some looked like they could have been Native Americans, dead before Europeans even knew this island existed."

Hugh grunted and shrugged awkwardly.

"That would be remarkable, but I do not see why it matters."

"I have never encountered a place this haunted that was this old, too. Hospitals and graveyards are prone to this. But there's nothing remarkable here. There's nothing here. That means the malevolence has been strong for a very long time. It doesn't need something else to bring death and the dead."

Hugh glanced at him as they walked. His face was too badly damaged to register much emotion, but there was confusion in his eyes.

"I do not understand what you are saying."

"I think this place is like a sponge. For hundreds and hundreds of years, it's just been sucking up the energy from every life it's taken. Whether it killed it, cannibals killed it, the King killed it, it doesn't matter. Everything goes back to the soil. Everything goes back into this island."

The pulse quickened around them, and the air grew hotter. The gusts of humid, rotten stench were thicker, and Shane put it out of his mind.

"There are places like this in the world. Houses, for instance. They grow powerful. They take on aspects of the dead within them. Cruelty. Bloodlust. They act as if they were living things," Shane continued.

"You think this island is alive? Like that Mallory woman did?"

"Not alive. Something else," Shane said.

"It cannot be dead. It was never alive," Hugh pointed out.

"Neither," Shane agreed. "It's more like a storm. The way a hurricane feeds on moisture, with hot air and cold air coming together until it releases a torrent. It's a force of nature."

The heartbeat thundered, and the stench was cloying. The air became harder to breathe, but Shane pushed onward.

Hugh's light dimmed almost imperceptibly. There was still enough by which to see and guide them through the tunnels, but it did not cover as much ground.

"I do not understand why you are telling me this. Does it make a difference in what we are about to do?"

"Not now. But later," Shane said. "It'll be important later."

Hugh grunted and seemed satisfied to end the conversation. Shane wasn't sure that what he had in mind would work, or if it would make a difference. He also wasn't sure they were going to survive to see the end of their mission. He planned on it, but he was not willing to make assurances for somebody else's safety, living or dead.

If Hugh made it through, then Shane would need to talk to him about what would happen going forward. But that would have to wait. Something about counting chickens before they hatched or making plans with a ghost before you knew he was going to survive what was coming.

"We are approaching another chamber." Hugh slowed down again.

Hugh entered the new chamber first, but Shane was only a step behind. The soft glow emitted by the ghost bathed the walls of a room that was smaller than the one they had been in, but it was still much wider than the tunnel.

The walls of the chamber were smooth, and there were markings upon them. Shane approached the nearest of them and Hugh joined him, bringing better illumination. They were not just markings; they were paintings on the wall in a red ocher color as well as what looked like black charcoal over carvings dug into the stone.

"Paintings," Hugh said.

"Cave paintings, yeah," Shane said.

The walls were full of art. It was done in a simple style, but easy enough to follow. The red paint showed trees with rudimentary, nearly stick-figure men around them. There were horses, and what looked like deer.

Another artwork showed taller figures with rectangular bodies and long, slender arms ending in pointy fingers. Their heads were nearly round, with eyes that were not colored in, just big, empty circles the color of the background rock.

There were symbols as well. Some were easy enough to figure out. One was clearly the sun, and another looked like a series of islands in the sea. Others were harder to understand. What looked like a sword with a blood groove buried in the ground, and the handle pointed up at the sun. There was a circle with a cross through it but not evenly placed at the ends of the cross and the other, smaller curve symbols attached to it.

"That's a stag." Hugh pointed at a deer with a massive rack of antlers. In the next image, a man was slaughtering the animal. In the final part of the triptych, the antlers were atop the head of a stick man who towered over the others. "And that's the King."

Hugh continued to investigate the paintings. Shane had stopped at the one depicting the stag and the King. He had a general sense of how old the art on the wall was. He had never heard of cave paintings in Maine, but there were petroglyph sites, places where rock carvings showed people and animals. He knew how old they were.

"You know what this means?" Shane asked.

"That the King killed the stag?" Hugh looked at the other paintings. He was focused on a large one on the opposite wall that depicted many bodies among the trees.

"The paintings, I mean. Do you know how old they are?" Shane clarified.

"I do not," Hugh admitted. "Old, I imagine."

"Very old," Shane corrected.

He was no expert on cave art but guessed they had to be thousands of years. It didn't matter how old. The King had been on the island for many centuries. The date kept getting pushed back.

Age didn't necessarily make a ghost more powerful. But it seemed like the King had spent his time refining his ability to kill. He had learned new ways to cause pain, and he had many victims to practice on. He didn't need to be powerful; he was knowledgeable.

Shane knew that killers had progression. There was enough literature out there on the subject. A serial killer might start by hurting animals and then graduate to a human victim and perform the task sloppily and haphazardly. Their second victim would be done more carefully. They would have developed a system by the time they reached the tenth victim.

Someone like the King—who had potentially killed hundreds, if not thousands, of people—would have gone beyond a system. He would have had time to explore every whim, every niche interest. That was why the ghosts on the trees were taken apart the way they had been. Why some had been dismembered, and others had been dissected.

The King wanted to experience new things. He wanted to inflict different kinds of pain. Maybe see how much a body could withstand. Many victims had probably died before the ones he displayed. Ones he had gotten overzealous with or who couldn't handle what he was doing as well as the others. It would have taken a lot of patience, a lot of time, and a lot of practice.

"The King has been here longer than you expected," Hugh said.

"Looks that way," Shane said.

"Are you afraid?"

Shane looked at the ghost. Hugh's expression was neutral. He was not making a dig or being confrontational; it was a legitimate question.

"No," Shane answered honestly. "Are you?"

"I am," the ghost admitted. "He is an expert in death, do you not think? A craftsman. My father made furniture, and he practiced his art for many years. But he was never as good as his father. He could never make the wood sing like my grandfather did. It was like he brought it to life when he carved. He once made a chair for the King of England, and they placed it in a guest room in the palace. He was an expert because he had devoted his whole life to his craft. And what of this King, then?"

"That's the thing about an expert." Shane touched one of the cave paintings that showed bodies among the trees. "If they go unchallenged for too long, they forget that they don't know everything."

"Yes," Hugh said. "Your confidence never wanes. I wonder if the irony is not lost on you."

Shane chuckled.

"I'm different from the King; don't worry."

"Are you certain? Misplaced confidence has been the death of many men."

"Exactly. I *know* I can die if I screw this up. My guess is that the King hasn't feared his destruction in several lifetimes. Probably doesn't even consider it possible. And that's going to ruin him."

"Never waning," Hugh said again.

"One of us has to be confident. You're getting depressing," Shane pointed out. "You're already dead. If you don't want to be deader, fight."

"That was my intention," Hugh said.

The thumping heartbeat stopped. The half-smile on Shane's face slipped away. He had locked eyes with Hugh, and neither moved or spoke for a moment. The hot air no longer blew through, and the stench of the cave was now just a low-lying, secondary feature. It was like the power had failed and everything had shut down.

A new sound emerged from the far side of the chamber. It was much quieter than the thumping heartbeat. Just a steady, slow rhythm of breathing. In and out, like someone meditating.

Hugh turned quickly to face the sound. The light he emitted did not extend that far into the chamber. The back wall, the farthest point from them where the sound was located, was concealed in darkness. The ghost took one step toward it, and then another. Shane moved with him, keeping an eye on their rear, in case the ghosts from earlier had rallied to attack.

The light shrank, pushed back by the dark. It was as though there was an invisible wall made of pure darkness that would not let the light in.

"Stop," Shane said before Hugh could take another step.

The breathing ended in one long, forceful exhale. Warm air rushed from the darkness, and a figure stepped into the edge of the light emanating from Hugh. It towered above Shane and the ghost, the multi-pointed antlers atop his head nearly scraping the ceiling of the cavern.

Shane could not see the King's face; it was still cast in shadow. This close to him, Shane saw the ghost's body for the first time, a patchwork of scars, many of them self-inflicted. He had cut patterns into his flesh like scarification tattoos. Other markings were clearly wounds achieved in battle. Some looked like they should have been life-threatening.

Hugh stepped back, and darkness swallowed the King again, but only for a moment. Torches blazed to life, a dozen of them wedged into holes carved in the walls as the King raised his hands. The flickering light filled the room and cast shadows of the King that danced and writhed in the light.

On the far wall was a pile of rubble that had been assembled into the crude shape of a chair, made of rock, bone, antlers, and wood.

They had found the throne room of the King.

CHAPTER 21

THE KING

The smell of smoke mingled with the smell of death in the room. It was a strange contrast to the stagnant, rotten, old smell of dead things. The King stood tall with his hands still raised dramatically.

Shane saw the ghost's body better in the light of the torches. Even though dirt and blood obscured most of his exposed flesh, he saw a patchwork of scars cut into the arms, chest, stomach, and legs. The King had carved complex patterns with a steady hand that covered his body. The scars were spirals, chevrons, and simple hash marks clustered in feathered patterns. There were no untouched spots.

Some of the cuts were simple slices; others had been deeper and wider. Segments of flesh had been peeled down to the muscle, and what remained was red and raw.

Before, in the woods, Shane had thought that hair obscured the King's face. He had a mane of long, wavy black hair that hung to his shoulders, but that was not the reason Shane couldn't see his face. The ghost wore a mask, the skull of a deer, affixed to his face.

The back of the skull had been cut away to allow a human face to fit into it. It looked to Shane like someone had slammed it onto the man's face while he was still alive. Shane saw where the animal bone had cut into the once-living flesh of the King's forehead just along the hairline. It was as though someone had fused animal and human skull into one.

Shane's first impression was that perhaps someone had done this to the King, but the scars on the ghost's body made him rethink that. The King might have done it to himself, forcing his head into the stag's skull on purpose.

The eyes in the skull were too wide set for a human to see out of effectively, but from where Shane stood, he saw one of the King's eyes looking at him. He gazed through the opening in the stag skull, and a single dark eye locked onto Shane. It was wide open, and it took Shane a moment to realize the King had no eyelids. Encircled by a fine pattern of red spider web-like veins, the iris was nearly black, making the pupil impossible to make out. It was as though the ghost's eye was just a pool of black in white, trailing hints of blood.

The king wore no crown upon his head. Shane now saw that the antlers, plucked from the head of a trophy stag long ago, had been implanted into the ghost's head through the stag skull he wore. Whether he had done it to himself or if it had been a cruel, final blow from whoever took his life, Shane couldn't guess. Whatever had transpired, the roots of the antlers had pierced the skull bone and were embedded securely in the ghost's head, the ends crusted over with black, scabby blood and what looked like broken bone and brain tissue.

"Why?" Hugh whispered softly, taking another step back.

The King turned his attention to the ghost. He flexed massive hands, large enough to cover a person's face like it was a softball. His nails were ragged, caked in dirt, and fractured on some fingers like he had been digging something by hand.

In person and up close, the King was even larger than he had seemed in the woods. He was easily more than seven feet tall, and his body was pure muscle beneath the multitude of scars. His limbs were too long, even for his size. His arms and fingers were slightly disproportionate like he had been afflicted with a condition that caused him to grow out of control.

Shane could only imagine how a man like that would have fit into a world a thousand years ago or more. He would have been seen as a monster and a freak. Combined with his violent disposition—if he'd had it while he was alive—everyone who saw him would have remembered him.

The King took a step forward, and Hugh moved back. Shane split the difference, moving ahead of his companion and putting himself between them.

"You got something—" Shane began a sarcastic quip, but the King turned on him, bending at the waist so they were face to face, and then, he roared.

Shane's jaw clenched almost involuntarily. He felt the bones in his body quake with a painful vibration. The cavern shook, the earth shook, and he heard it rumbling beneath the sound that came out of the ghost's mouth. It was like nothing he had ever heard, funneled through the skull of the stag. It was so much louder than it had been in the woods, and so much more intense.

He wanted to move, wanted to strike out at the ghost, cover his own ears, or something. But Shane found himself frozen, the vibration through his bones and muscles preventing him from doing anything. Pain radiated across every inch of his being. It was like being caught in the blast of a jet engine without the heat, just an intense force bearing down on him that he could do nothing about.

The sound felt like it would never end. Shane could not concentrate on the King, the cave, or anything. The feeling was nearly unbearable. His heart beat rapidly, he could only breathe in shallow breaths, and his stomach felt like it was being squeezed in a powerful vise.

His body lurched and spasmed, and he vomited on the stone in front of his feet. That single eye, lidless and intense, stared at him through the stag's skull. Shane felt his legs wobble.

The shaking in his legs grew too intense, and Shane collapsed. He couldn't move his arms quickly enough—the rest of his body still felt frozen—and he simply fell onto his side, lying on the floor as the endless bellow from the King shook him to his core.

Shane's rage had gone from a simmer to a furious boil as he fought the paralysis that rendered him inert. That he could be so easily disabled, to be at the mercy of the thing in front of him, was an insult. It angered him. He was defenseless, and the King knew it.

Above him, the King produced the blade of bone that Hugh had told him about. It was long and thin, and the color of old ivory. The handle was wrapped in a pale-colored leather, with the straps crisscrossed around it. He leaned closer to Shane, turning his head so that Shane could no longer see the eye, only the stag skull obscured behind a veil of hair.

With his free hand, the King reached out and grabbed Shane by the top of his head. His hands were so large that he could palm Shane's skull and lift him into a kneeling position. Shane thought he was unusually warm for a ghost. Cold, but not nearly as cold as he should have been. His hand squeezed Shane's head, applying pressure and forcing him to turn as he leveled the point of the bone blade with Shane's left eye.

The King held his blade steady, millimeters from Shane's eye while the endless roar continued. All he had to do was push forward with barely any effort and Shane would have been blinded. But he held it, his arm motionless, and his grip firm. He held strong, only threatening the attack, not following through.

Shane realized that this was what he wanted. This was what the King thrived on. Not death, but pain. Fear and pain were what he desired. He wanted Shane to be terrified, but he would not be so lucky.

Though Shane could barely move, he had no fear that the ghost would blind him. Not that he didn't think it wouldn't happen, he was just not afraid of it. His anger was too strong now. The only thing Shane focused on was what he would do when he regained control of his body.

He saw weak points across the King's exposed frame. His flesh had been peeled away too deeply around his ribs, and bone was exposed under his arms. If Shane could get a hand in there, he could pull apart the ghost's ribs and collapse his chest.

From below, as the King leaned over him, Shane saw where the bone of the stag's skull had been embedded around the ghost's head. The underside was open, and Shane saw part of the King's jaw. It would be easy enough to get his hand hooked under the edge of the animal skull and tear the entire thing off the spirit's face. One quick swipe, and he would expose the King's true face, already weakened by the skull and the antlers, and vulnerable.

The tip of the bone blade came closer, almost touching the lens of Shane's eye. He tried to move his hands and lift his arms, but it felt like every muscle in his body had contracted at the same time and refused to relax. He wanted to lay into the ghost, he wanted to yell at him, tear the hand from his wrist, and stab him in the gut with the blade. He wanted to do something. Anything. But he could not.

Hugh's body crashed into the King, tackling him just above the waist. The paralyzing roar cut off immediately, and Shane went limp and loose as he slumped to the floor. He breathed deeply, finally able to take a proper breath and fill his lungs, and then he sat up as quickly as he could.

His head swam, and his pulse raced. He forced himself to continue taking deep breaths as he regained his bearings.

Hugh was atop the King, landing punches on the exposed ribs Shane had observed just moments earlier. He fought with a fury that Shane had not seen from the ghost. He was not as cautious as he normally was, and not as strategic by any means. Instead, both fists pummeled the other ghost's midsection, cracking ribs with loud, popping sounds as though he intended to break into the King's chest cavity. The attack had surprised the larger ghost, but the effect was short-lived.

The King grabbed Hugh about the neck, pulling the smaller ghost away as he got to his feet. Shane watched as the King held Hugh at arm's length like he was inspecting him. Then, he jerked his arm upward. Hugh flew, vanishing through the cavern ceiling. The toss looked forceful. Shane could only guess how high Hugh would have been thrown, unhindered by the effects of stone or other impediments, but he was gone now. The King only had Shane to deal with.

Shane forced himself to his feet, still feeling lightheaded and unsteady, but doing his best not to show it. He spit out the taste of vomit and balled his hands into fists.

"Well, come on, asshole. Let me tear off one of those horns and gut you with it," he said.

The King ran toward Shane.

CHAPTER 22
DEATH AT HAND

Shane choked. The King's hand squeezed his neck as he ran the final few steps to the cavern wall. He held Shane as he had held Hugh, grasped firmly in one hand and dangling above the ground like he was a rag doll.

When they reached the wall, the King slammed Shane against the stone, holding him at eye level. With the height difference, Shane was a foot off the ground, pinned against the rocky surface as the one, wild eye peered at him through the skull mask.

Shane gripped the ghost's wrist with both of his hands. He applied pressure to twist the King's hand away, but it was like moving stone. He adjusted his grip, hooking his fingers under the ghost's thumb and opening his hand. Even with as much pressure as he could apply, he barely got the digit to budge.

He could hear the King breathing, the pointless sound coming from inside the skull over the dead man's face. The cavern was alive again, beating with the sound of Shane's elevated pulse. It was a reminder in his ears of the stress he was under and the strain on his body as he breathed and worked to keep the ghost's grip loose enough to take in air.

The blade returned. Shane fended off the King, taking hold of his other wrist and forcing it back. The ghost pushed forward, and the cold point of the bone knife bit into Shane's flesh just below his cheekbone.

Shane winced, clenching his teeth. The King dragged the blade down, pushing deeper until the point scraped against Shane's teeth. He sliced open a gash about two inches long into Shane's face and held the blade there, pushing harder, threatening to break the tooth it rested against.

Blood filled Shane's mouth. The King tapped the tip of the knife against Shane's tooth again and again, each time a little harder. He operated with the curiosity of a child burning ants with a magnifying glass. His eye was fixated on Shane's wound as though he had never harmed anyone or seen blood before.

Shane spit at the ghost, but it passed through him harmlessly and splattered on the floor. Slowly, with a twist of his wrist, the King pulled the knife from the wound he had created, enlarging it briefly as the blade spun.

The blade disappeared, and Shane did not see what the King had done with it beyond a flourish of his fingers. He held Shane firmly with his other hand and then reached toward his face. Shane kicked at him but couldn't reach. He beat at the ghost's arm again and again, until the King slammed him hard against the wall. Shane's vision swam, and for a moment, he saw only white.

While he cleared his mind, a new pain burned through his face. The King had inserted a finger into the hole he had made in Shane's cheek. Broad, blunt, and cold, he probed at the wound, pushing into Shane's mouth.

With his jaws parted, Shane kept up the struggle as the ghost's finger plunged deeper into his mouth. When it was far enough, he bit down as hard as he could. A hissing sound escaped the King's mouth from within his bone mask. Shane shook his head, clamping his jaws shut as tightly as he could until he felt something snap.

The end of the ghost's finger broke off in his mouth. It only took a moment to fade from existence, but for a brief time, the thick bulk of it rested on his tongue like a cold slab of meat.

He expected retaliation. Some kind of reaction from the ghost. His hope was that the King would drop him, letting rage overtake rationality and make a mistake that Shane could capitalize on. Instead, he held Shane fast against the wall and stared at his own hand.

The pressure on Shane's neck increased until he could barely breathe. The King turned his hand over and back again, inspecting the missing fingertip on his right forefinger. Shane saw the stag skull tilt, and the ghost brought his hand closer to himself. It was like he saw something remarkable and was enthralled by it.

Something about losing the finger fascinated the ghost. Shane did not know how long it would last, but he couldn't let the distraction go to waste.

He gripped the ghost's wrist as tightly as he could, braced himself, and swung his feet forward, compressing his core and lifting his body. The momentum of his feet carried him forward, and he wrapped his legs around the King's arm below the shoulder. The spirit retreated just as Shane expected him to. At the same moment, Shane pulled back his leg and kicked forward as hard as he could.

The heel of his boot smashed into the skull attached to the spirit's head. Bone splintered, and Shane made contact with the King's true face underneath. The hand on his neck released him, and they fell to the ground together.

Shane landed hard but rolled onto all fours and got up as quickly as he could. The only advantage he would get was surprise. The King was faster and stronger than him.

He rushed at the ghost, lifted a leg, and aimed for the spirit's knee. If Shane could cripple him, if he could keep him on the ground, he would have a chance. His leg was up, and the heel of his boot was perfectly placed over the scarred leg of the King. And then, his muscles seized.

The King whipped his head toward Shane, his shaggy, loose-hanging black hair flying back and exposing the full skull attached to his face. The left side was broken away and Shane saw part of the face underneath. He saw a lipless mouth, teeth that had been filed to points, and a tongue covered in ulcers as the fierce bellow shook the cavern.

Shane tumbled backward as the King threw a poorly aimed but vicious punch, taking him square in the gut. He was still on his knees when he lashed out, more from anger than anything else, but Shane could not defend himself.

The fist hit him like a baseball bat and he was helpless to do anything but tumble back and skid across the stone floor of the cavern, coming to rest under one of the torches fixed to the wall.

Shane stopped with a groan, his jaw locked shut as he felt stone dig into his sides and back. The King slowly got to his feet, still raging and roaring like a chorus of beasts with the sound that set every muscle in Shane's body on fire.

Again, the King seemed distracted. For a moment, Shane thought he was going to storm toward him and attack him again, but the King caught sight of his hand and marveled again at the missing finger. The roar died in his throat. Shane was freed from the paralysis that had overtaken him, and he went limp.

The process of his muscles relaxing was not quick. It took him a moment to regain control of himself, roll over onto his hands and knees, and shake off the tingling sensation that ran through his body. But his efforts to get control, regain his footing, and prepare for another round were not as pressing as he imagined they'd need to be. The King made no move. He was still caught up in the finger joint that Shane had bitten off, staring as though hypnotized.

From a tunnel beyond the ramshackle throne at the head of the room, the beating sound thundered through the cavern. It sounded like a hundred bass drums, like the island had a heart that was right behind the reach of the torchlight.

The festering, hot stink of the air from the depths rolled over Shane. The island increased its onslaught, picking up the slack for the King and his momentary distraction. But even as it took Shane's attention, the King was roused from what he was doing as well, lifting his head and shaking it, setting the mop of hair moving before he lowered his hand and then turned the skull-masked face toward Shane.

"Next time, I take the whole hand," Shane said.

The King growled and then ran. He was bent low, the fingers on both hands lightly grazing the ground and giving him the appearance of running on all fours. He lowered his head as Shane backed up, but there was nowhere to go. Pressed against the wall, the King crashed into him with enough force to shake the cavern walls. Dust and stone fell from the ceiling, and one of the torches tumbled from the wall, snuffing itself as it rolled away.

The antlers on the King's head sank into the stone on either side of Shane's torso, piercing it as easily as drywall. One of the lower points, no bigger than a thumb, dug into Shane's stomach, puncturing through his jacket and into his flesh.

Shane cried out in pain but lifted his arm, slamming his elbow down onto the ghost's head. He heard the bone mask crunch but only succeeded in cracking the bone, not breaking it. The advantage was lost a moment later as the King pulled away harshly, grabbing Shane with both hands and throwing him across the room.

Bone and rock broke apart and tumbled around Shane's body as he crashed into the throne against the far wall, breaking it. He felt his lungs deflate as his chest compressed. It was like being hit by a car.

The loose construction, held together with clay and sticks, shattered, burying Shane in the rubble. He landed on the floor, face-first on the uncomfortably warm stone, and remained still.

Shane gasped for air. It felt like he had a massive weight on his chest even though there was only a small amount of rubble. The force of the blow had compressed his lungs, and he struggled to even get a small amount of air back.

The King stomped toward him, charging like the stag whose head he wore, scooping Shane up and slamming him back into the wall.

Shane gasped, wheezing as he took a breath and the ghost held his throat. His windpipe squeezed even as the King pulled his arm back and formed his hand into a fist.

The gigantic ghost punched Shane square in the chest, and spots danced before his eyes. He couldn't get any air in.

He heard a faint growl from the skull. The King's ragged-looking mouth was set in a tense grimace, his sharpened teeth clenched, and his muscles strained. Shane did not think the ghost's effort made it look so strained. Instead, strangely, it seemed to be restraint.

The room dimmed, and Shane beat at the King's arm, digging his nails into the ghostly flesh to get free. The sound of the island's beating heart stopped. The King's one wild eye loomed close as the ghost turned his head, an antler brushing Shane's cheek as he stared into Shane's eye. Shane recognized the gaze in the red-rimmed, manic eyes of the dead man.

He wanted to watch Shane's life slip away. He wanted a front-row seat.

CHAPTER 23

LAST STAND

Shane's nails peeled strips of flesh from the King's forearm, but the ghost did not care. His grip remained tight. The antler scraped the side of Shane's head as that one eye bore into his as though looking into his soul.

He tried to pull the skull off the ghost's head. He kicked the monstrous ghost in the chest and stomach. He tried everything he could think of, and then he fell to the ground.

Shane landed in the same pile of rocks that had collapsed on him before. His throat felt like it had been folded in on itself. He grabbed his neck, holding it, and massaging the bruised tissue as he struggled to draw in air now that he was free from the King's grip.

His first breath was a slow wheeze that felt like he was taking it in through a narrow straw. The next breath came easier. He lay on the ground with his eyes closed to remain calm and focused. He needed to keep his wits about him. He needed to make his throat and his lungs work, or he would black out soon. He would not survive if he could not remain conscious.

Even if he couldn't breathe, he couldn't forget about the King. He couldn't leave himself vulnerable to another attack if he could avoid it. He didn't even know why the ghost had let him go.

Shane pushed up off the ground, getting into a sitting position and leaning against the wall as he drew in his first, proper breath in what seemed like minutes. The figure standing before him, leaning down and reaching out, was not the King.

"Can you walk?" Frank held out his hand. In his other, he held a wrought-iron bar.

Shane smiled, choking out a laugh.

"You got him?" Shane's voice was strained.

"Oh," Frank said, looking at the bar in his hand. "Yeah. Hit him across the back. Seemed like you needed a hand."

"I did," Shane agreed.

He hated that Hugh had been right about the King. He was too strong. He was fast and powerful and, aside from a morbid fascination with a severed finger joint, nothing distracted him.

Frank took Shane's arm and helped hoist him to his feet.

"Where the hell did you come from?" Shane asked, still breathing deeply.

"There." Frank pointed to the tunnel. "I came looking for you after we left the island."

Shane raised an eyebrow, and Frank nodded.

"Yeah. Weird story. You came back, or someone posing as you, and we got everyone on the boats and left. And then the fake you vanished. I came back after I've secured everyone on the mainland."

"I've been busy," Shane said.

"Looks like. Should we leave, do you think?"

"Yes. Yeah… how far back the way you came?"

Frank looked at the tunnel and shook his head.

"I've been down here for two hours, maybe? If he's down here with us, I'd rather find a faster way if you know one."

"There." Shane pointed across the cavern to the entrance he'd used with Hugh.

"I don't mean to rush you. It looks like you need time to rest—"

"I'm fine." Shane shook his head. He wasn't, but he would be. After all, Frank was right. Staying in the cavern was asking for death. The King would be back soon enough.

Frank started moving first, and Shane joined him quickly, looking back over his shoulder. The torches of the room were still lit, flickering and casting shadows, but the smell and sound had vanished. The cave was cold, and their footfalls echoed ominously off the stone.

Frank produced a flashlight from his bag and directed the beam down the tunnel as they left the chamber.

"So, is everyone off the island now?" Shane asked.

"The residents are all back on the mainland. The boats were right where we left them."

"So, they were never moved?" Shane asked. "Or did someone bring them back?"

"I'm leaning more toward an illusion," Frank answered. "We never did check the dock up close. And the fake you that appeared was very convincing."

"Fake me," Shane repeated. "You talked to it?"

"The evacuation took several hours, and you were there the whole time. Or it seemed like you at first."

Shane watched the tunnel for signs of the ghosts he had fought earlier, but nothing even moved in the shadows.

"At first?"

"Didn't have your charm," Frank explained.

Shane chuckled and nodded.

"You had to fight it?"

"No, which was odd. It helped us all leave. And then it just vanished. It wanted us gone. Maybe as a trade. Us for you."

Shane grunted. He hadn't expected that. An illusory version of himself that aided everyone's escape seemed needless. Generous, even, if it wasn't actively causing trouble.

"It made it clear to me that I did not need to come back to the island," Frank added.

"Yet here you are," Shane replied.

"Can't let sinister doppelgangers start telling me what to do. But what about you? What happened to Hugh?"

"Don't know," Shane said. "He got thrown out of the cave when the fight began. The King… I don't know what to do to put him down."

They walked in silence for a moment, following the beam of yellow light. From the depths of the tunnels behind them, a low, slow thumping began again. The pulse had returned.

Frank stopped, turning to look back the way they had come.

"Don't worry. It does this," Shane explained. "He's coming back."

"Sounds like something to worry about," Frank said.

"We need to get outside. If I have more room, I might be able to think of something to do. Confined in a closed space with him was a bad idea. I need to come at this from another angle. I can't fight him with brute strength. There has to be something else we can do."

"There's two of us now; that has to count for something," Frank pointed out.

"Three," came another voice as the flashlight illuminated the figure crouched on the tunnel floor in front of them.

Hugh was waiting, looking more ragged than when Shane had seen him last. More meat had been torn from his bones. A length of flesh on his torso dangled to the ground, hanging from the thinnest, twisted strand of skin.

"Hugh! What happened?" Frank asked.

The ghost rose to a standing position and glanced at his body.

"Others were waiting for me when I surfaced. It took some time to get back." He looked from Frank to Shane before adding, "I feared you would not survive."

"I made it. But it was touch and go for a minute," Shane replied.

"I see that."

The ghost gestured to Shane's cheek and the hole the King had pierced through it. Shane had nearly forgotten about it. The remnants of the pain in his chest, and the burn in his throat and lungs when he breathed was at the front of his mind.

"What happened to him?" Hugh looked back the way Shane and Frank had come.

"Reprieve." Frank held up the iron bar.

"Then we do not have long," the ghost said.

The thumping sound of the pulse from deep in the earth continued, shaking the walls of the tunnel as if to accentuate his point.

Hugh turned and began to lead the way out. The soft glow around the ghost's body returned, allowing them to see more of the area than Frank's flashlight did.

They reached the cavern that had been full of ghosts and found the space empty.

"You cleared this?" Shane asked.

"No," Hugh said. "They have retreated somewhere."

"I assume you mean *them*." Frank pointed the beam of his flashlight toward one of the branching tunnels. A trio of ghosts waited at the tunnel entrance, none of which Shane recognized from their first run-through.

Frank moved the beam of light to reveal more spirits ducked out of the reach of Hugh's illumination. There were many more than had been there when Shane arrived.

Shane grunted, the sound coming out more like a growl with his strained throat.

"Thought we learned this lesson already," he said to the looming spirits.

The pulse drummed harder and, back the way they came, the King roared, briefly drowning out all other sounds.

Shane felt his muscles tense, but it didn't have the paralyzing effect it had up close. He cursed and then glanced at Frank, whose eyes were wide as he let out a shuddering exhale.

"That felt like an ice bath. My muscles—" he began.

"I know. You don't want it face to face," Shane said. "Move."

Frank ran, and the moment his feet were in motion, it was as though a switch had gone off. The ghosts in the tunnels around the cavern surged forward into Hugh's light. Shane ran with him, taking the tunnel that led toward the surface with Hugh following behind.

The pulse quickened to a thundering staccato. The ghosts from the cavern howled, laughed, and screamed with rage. A deafening cacophony followed them, the rage of dozens of dead licking at their heels.

Frank nearly stumbled and fell over a segment of loose rock. Shane caught his arm, practically dragging him back to his feet, and the two of them continued running. The ground was too uneven and too unpredictable for either to achieve a good pace. The ghosts behind were gaining ground, and Shane was too aware of how much space separated them from the exit. They would not get out in time.

"Are we going to make it?" Frank asked.

"No," Shane said. "We need to fight."

The King raged again, the sound shaking loose dust and debris from the tunnel ceiling. He was closer now, much closer than he had been, and gaining ground.

The heartbeat sounded like it was coming from the walls, the floor, and the entire tunnel. They might as well have been traveling inside a beating heart for the way it encompassed them.

The King's anger seemed to be absorbed by the other ghosts. The others became frenzied in response to his bellow. Some clawed their way along the walls, running sideways and filling the space like a swarm of insects.

"They are going to catch us if you cannot run faster." Hugh pushed past Shane and Frank to take the lead, illuminating the path more clearly. It helped only marginally. Running on uneven ground was not something that got much better even when you could see where you were going, especially at a frenzied pace.

"Hold that thought."

Frank had reached into his pocket and, though still running, appeared distracted for a moment until he pulled out a closed fist, dropping glittering fragments of metal as he went. Shane saw that his hand was full of iron filings and watched as the other man turned, mid-run, and extended his arm as though throwing a baseball.

Metal shavings glittered like stardust in the soft light cast by Hugh. They scattered through the narrow passage, bouncing off the walls and floor. The ghosts in pursuit fizzled, popping out of existence until only a few remained.

The bare handful of ghosts that avoided the iron stopped their pursuit, suddenly stripped of the boldness in the face of their drastically shrunken numbers.

Frank turned back and picked up the pace, matching Shane as they fled. The heartbeat of the cave had yet to subside, and a repetitive thump discordant with the heartbeat approached quickly in the dark. Shane knew the King was running after them. His feet didn't need to make a sound as he stomped through the tunnels, but it was all part of the show.

They made it around a curve in the tunnel, exposing the tooth-filled cave ahead. The night sky waited for them. The sun had yet to rise, and would maybe never rise again as long as the King was still around. But the ambient light of the night was within reach.

Frank took in the view of the cave entrance for the first time. The jagged, fang-like spikes curved down, making it look just as much like a mouth from the inside as it did from the outside.

"Keep running," Shane advised.

The King roared again. He was close. Too close.

"How do we fight this thing?" Frank asked, breathing heavily as he pushed himself. They broke free of the tunnel and entered the mouth of the cave. The footfalls of the King were past the previous cavern by now, past where they had scattered the iron at the other ghosts.

"I don't know," Shane said. "Whatever we can do. But out of this place. In the open."

It was too dangerous to fight in the cave. It gave the King too many advantages, and too many chances to use the surrounding stone as a weapon. He already had a height, reach, and strength advantage. They didn't need to give him close quarters to make it easier.

The beating heart stopped. A new sound replaced it. Rocks fell from the ceiling amid plumes of dust and pebbles. The stony fangs began to descend, and Shane swore loudly.

The mouth was closing.

CHAPTER 24
SURFACING

"Is he really *this* powerful?" Frank yelled, covering his head as stones rained down upon them.

They were twenty yards from the cave entrance at most. They were so close. Shane had been confident they would get outside before they were forced to square off with the King, but the island was not done with them.

"It's the island. It's feeding off him. His rage fuels it. And I think it fuels him," Shane yelled back, dodging a rock the size of his head. It was getting hard to breathe again. He was certain he had bruised if not broken ribs, and his throat burned fiercely as he drew in the freezing air.

"How is that even possible?" Frank asked.

Shane gasped for air and ignored the question. The sharp columns of stone were descending as quickly as the structure of the cave would allow.

Behind them, the thundering sound of the King's footsteps were getting louder. He entered the chamber with another fearsome roar, and Shane felt his muscles stiffen to the point that he stumbled and nearly fell.

"Keep running and do not stop," Hugh shouted at him and Frank as he turned back.

"My God..." Frank whispered, craning his head back and getting his first good look at the King from the front.

Shane grabbed Frank's arm to get him to focus on getting to the mouth of the cave. They still had time.

Hugh met the King, diving low and tackling the larger spirit by colliding with his knee. Shane got a glimpse of them falling in a tangle and he ran faster. If the ghost was sacrificing himself to save Shane and Frank, the least they could do was fulfill his wishes and get out of the cave.

The stone fangs reached the floor of the cave, the tips shattering and spraying shrapnel. Shane raised an arm to shield his face and ducked to avoid the roof of the mouth as it came down hard, crushing the teeth to rubble.

Shane and Frank tumbled out into the night, Frank stumbling in the snow and falling as the cave collapsed shut behind them.

The earth shook as Shane came to a stop. The cave had vanished. The sound, the smell, everything. In its place were a handful of wooden cabins covered in snow. They were back in the village, standing outside of Alina's cabin in ankle-deep snow.

He turned quickly in a full circle, still breathing deeply to fill his lungs. The ramshackle cabins were there as well, and the Great Hall, and the greenhouse, though the windows were broken. It was not the village of the past where Shane had spent the night, it was the village of the present.

"How did we get here?" Frank asked, getting back to his feet.

"The island controls itself. It has since we got here," Shane answered. "Been playing with us all this time."

"This is real, then?" Frank asked.

He reached for the green door to Alina's cabin. The doorknob squeaked as he turned it, and the door fell open. The inside, though cast in shadow, was disheveled. Shelves of Alina's artwork were knocked over, some of them on the floor. It looked like she had ransacked the place in a hurry before leaving.

"Real as anything here needs to be," Shane said.

Something within the cabin shuffled in the dark near the back wall. Frank took a step back, and a shape came forward on all fours. Shane saw the hands and the arms first, noticing where chunks of flesh and meat had been torn away. The wounds were so deep in some places that they revealed bone. It looked like Hugh, and the other cannibal spirits that they had fought and destroyed. This body was too slender, though.

The sky above them had opened. It was still dark, but the clouds had parted. Moonlight allowed them to see; an intentional gesture by the island. Shane reminded himself that everything was happening for a reason. Maple Grove was like a snow globe, a controlled environment in which nothing happened by accident.

The mutilated thing crawled into a patch of moonlight, lifting a face that was stripped of skin from the cheekbones down.

"Alina…" Frank said softly.

Half of her blonde hair had been ripped from her skull, the wounds exposing smooth, white bone stained with blood. Her back was open, flayed to the spine. Everything looked fresh and was still wet and dripping.

The way the skin had been removed made her face look almost like a clown mouth, with a giant red slash that curved up to the left and right. Her lipless mouth clacked as she chomped her teeth. Her eyes remained clear, focused intently on Shane and Frank.

"She got back to Maine. I took her there myself," Frank whispered, still in disbelief.

"You also saw me then," Shane reminded him.

Their words brought out another spirit, scuttling out of the dark on nearly fleshless legs. Shane didn't recognize this one, the face of a young man whose eyes had been plucked from his head. Frank's reaction told him he knew who it was though.

"Jackson."

Shane had only seen the young man in a photo, and he was alive and healthy, smiling for the camera. This thing was thin and torn apart, a mutilated and degraded version of what he had been.

Something crunched in the snow behind them, and Shane turned. Another ghost was crawling toward them on three limbs, its right arm missing. Even with serious damage to the face, Shane recognized it as Blaine.

More crawled out from the shadows, out of the open doors of cabins, and across the rooftops. Mallory was there, Brandon, Clint, Lonnie, and everyone that Shane had met in the village. All the villagers were there, their bodies sliced apart, chewed up, and covered in cuts, bite marks, bruises, and more.

Unlike the ones that Shane had fought already, the villagers looked fresh, like they had just died moments earlier. Their wounds bled freely, trailing bright red through the snow, lit by the silver light of the moon.

"Can they harm us?" Frank held the iron rod like a knife.

"That cave was going to crush us. These? I don't know. Did the other me do anything?"

Shane saw the subtle change of expression on Frank's face.

"He carried bags. Untied rope. Put a hand on my shoulder once. Felt real."

Shane grunted, watching the village of the dead come closer like pack animals working together on their approach to prey.

"Then I think we need to be cautious."

"Cautiousssssssssssssss!"

The word was hissed from the back of the pack. Mallory stood on unsteady legs, her thighs chewed away. Her lower lip had been peeled down, dragging the skin from her chin halfway down her neck. Her eyes, nose, and ears bled freely, dripping slowly but consistently.

The short woman crept forward, her arms swaying strangely, and her body swaying left and right, like she might fall at any moment.

"What cautionnnnnnn?"

"Mallory, you look lovely as ever." Shane circled away from the cabin that housed Alina and Jackson, keeping as many of the other illusions in front of him as he could.

"You got ussssssssss alllll killed," Mallory hissed.

Her head wobbled left and right when she spoke, as though she couldn't hold it upright. Her voice was off, deeper than it had been, and gravelly. She also seemed taller than she had been when she was alive. The illusion was convincing enough, but Shane was not sure why the island had chosen to make the strange changes to her. Perhaps it was just overwhelmed. There had to be a limit to how much energy the place could expend, and how convincing it could make its lies look, as it juggled so many at once.

Shane laughed, a surprised and gruff one given the state of his throat. It had taken him by surprise.

"Guilt? You're guilting me? You almost have the look down, but psychology is not your strong suit," he said. "Shouldn't have expected a pile of rocks and maple syrup to do any better."

Mallory's teeth chattered, and Blaine stood.

"I should have killed you when I had the chance," he croaked, his voice far too deep.

"Yeah, probably," Shane agreed. "Shoulda done some target practice."

"Shane," Frank said.

Shane glanced at him. Frank was backing away slowly as Alina crept from her cabin.

"You good?"

"I'm just thinking, if this is the island, if we have a direct link to this place to communicate, then maybe this is a real chance to learn about it. Is it alive? Is it… sentient? Does it want something?"

Shane shrugged.

"Hey, what do you want?" he asked the thing that looked like Alina.

"Death." Her voice was like the slither of a snake.

"Jesus." Shane shook his head. "Shake some chains in the attic while you're at it."

"There must be something," Frank shouted into the darkness, addressing the island. "All this effort. All this power. You must have been here for a long time."

"Since you left us to die," Alina hissed dryly.

"Since you killed ussssssssss," Mallory added.

"You let us all die!" Blaine said.

All the ghosts began talking, blaming, and lamenting something that had never happened to most of them. Shane understood what Frank was doing. The sentiment made sense, but Frank didn't understand what he was dealing with. Shane couldn't say he fully understood what he was dealing with either, but they were not ghosts, not real ones anyway. And the island was never going to talk to them. It was never going to share its point of view or intentions. It didn't have those things.

In Shane's mind, the island was much more like a Venus flytrap. It could kill, and it reacted when it had prey, but there was no thought process behind it. He understood Frank's desire to give it human attributes, to recognize things that seemed too complex to be done by chance. But he did not think that was the case.

"These people didn't die," Frank still tried to get through. "You know that. You helped them escape. You helped me get them out of here. You must have wanted them to live."

"I want you to die, Frank," Jackson said.

The ghost was on his feet, steadying himself in the doorway to Alina's cabin. His stomach had been torn open, and the flesh was laid out over his thighs like an apron. Many of his organs were missing, but his intestines had flopped to the ground and were dragging behind him. Blood still dripped from his rib cage into the cavernous wound in a constant flow.

"Jackson," Frank said with a sigh. "I—"

"It's not Jackson," Shane reminded him. "None of these are ghosts. None of them know what you're saying."

Frank sighed as the thing that looked like Jackson shambled toward him, its guts dragging through the snow.

"I know," Frank said quietly.

He swung the wrought-iron rod and smashed the side of the illusion's head. It staggered for a moment as though the hit had been real, as though it were a real person, but a heartbeat later, it was gone.

"You killed us!" Clint yelled furiously, in a voice more commanding than anything Clint had mustered in real life. His chest had been cracked, and it looked as though his heart had been removed.

"I don't care," Shane replied. He approached the taller man, adjusting an iron ring on his finger, and took a swing. His fist made contact with Clint's chin, and it felt like he was punching a pillow, different from when hitting a real ghost.

Clint vanished, and the other illusions hissed and screamed and threatened, but none attacked. Shane waded through all of them, pushing past those that crouched and scowled with tattered, bloody faces. They swiped at him, lunged, and made threats, but nothing touched him.

"Spread yourself too thin." Shane backhanded Blaine and made the illusion vanish. "You still have limits."

"You will diiiiiiiiiiiiie," Mallory growled.

Her words were drowned out then, consumed and overwhelmed by a much louder, more familiar sound. The roar of the King.

Not in the distance but in the village.

CHAPTER 25
LONG LIVE THE KING

The illusions were gone. Only the King remained in the village with Shane and Frank. He ran at full speed toward the two men.

Frank ducked aside into Alina's now-empty cabin while Shane backed up. The King's long legs covered the distance in seconds. He ducked his head low, and the antlers atop his head slipped under Shane's arms, with several points digging into his chest and sides.

Shane's body lurched back under the force of the King's attack, skidding backward in the snow. He grabbed hold of each antler at the base where it protruded from the skull fixed onto the King's head. The ghost thundered forward like a bull, pushing Shane toward the nearest cabin wall.

With gritted teeth, Shane tensed and pushed down as hard as he could. He felt the antlers give way, and the King roared again. Not the paralyzing sound he had used before, but an enraged noise, a surprised noise as something snapped inside the bone mask that covered his face.

The King stopped and straightened his back, standing upright and lifting Shane off the ground with him. He was strong, but not so strong that he could do such a thing with no effort. Shane kept a grip on the antlers, even as gravity pushed him down harder onto the points that dug into his padded jacket. He felt two digging into his flesh, but he ignored them as he focused his efforts on the base of the antlers.

Hands like vises took hold of Shane's forearms and tried to pull him away. He refused to let go. Instead, he focused his grip and then kicked out, the toe of his boot coming up under the stag skull and smashing into the King's jaw from underneath.

The King's head snapped back, dragging Shane with it and out of the ghost's grip. His body shook, and he staggered backward. The antlers snapped again, and Shane felt them give way. Both broke simultaneously, and Shane fell to the ground in front of the ghost, still holding them in his hands.

A new scream emerged from behind the bone mask that the King wore. There was rage there, but the pitch was off. It was unhinged and panicked. It sounded to Shane like primal fear.

The ghost clutched his head, giant hands grasping the animal skull and covering the holes where the antlers had once been. Shane moved quickly. His feet had barely touched the ground as he rose, hands outstretched toward the giant ghost. The antlers had not yet vanished as a result of being detached from their host. He drove them deep into the King's inner thighs, one on either side where his legs attached at the groin, plunging the deepest point into the flesh and forcing them up with every bit of strength he had.

Embedded in the King's flesh, the antlers stayed where they were rather than fading from existence like severed ghost limbs might do. The giant spirit wailed in anger and what sounded like pain, even though Shane knew he couldn't feel such a thing.

He threw a punch, aiming for the ghost's ribs, the iron ring still firmly affixed on his finger. He would send the King back where he came from and let the spirit deal with the antlers wedged in his legs.

Shane swung hard, his arm curving toward the ghost in a strong right hook. The skull-covered head looked down, that one eye glaring at him again as the King's hand snapped out and caught Shane by the wrist. He stopped the punch before it made contact, keeping him from being banished by the iron.

Frank had emerged from Alina's cabin and had crept behind the ghost. With the wrought-iron rod held high, he brought it down toward the King's back, but the ghost knew he was coming this time.

Twisting his body around, the ghost swung Shane, lifting him from the ground and slamming him into Frank, knocking the other man over. He did not loosen his grip. Instead, the ghost took Shane's other wrist, preventing him from fighting back, and held him up.

The King kicked Frank in the gut where he lay on the ground, causing the man to double over and retch. He carried Shane to the nearest cabin, the antlers lodged in his legs clicking together but not slowing him, and pressed the living man against the wall, keeping both wrists pinned in place.

A scuttling, sloppy, wet sound filled the village. The ghosts from the cavern had crawled up through the snow. Their numbers were small at first, but more and more appeared, flooding the visible landscape.

Shane struggled in the King's grip. He kicked out, but the ghost held him at arm's length, and his size made it hard for Shane to make contact. He scraped the end of his boot against the ghost's exposed chest and ribs but with barely any force. Certainly nothing debilitating, nothing that the ghost would even notice.

"Frank!" Shane yelled to get his friend's attention.

The other man was still curled on the ground. Shane could see that he had spit up blood, suffering some internal injuries from the kick he had received. He was still moving, but his recovery was slow. The waterlogged, rotten spirits were all around him. They would be on him soon enough, and on the ground, he would have little chance to gain leverage for a counterattack, iron weapons or not.

"Frank, get up!"

The King shook him and snorted, a rush of air coming out of the end of the skull mask, cold and foul. His one eye was fixed on Shane's.

"GEEE SAHHH NIIIT."

The voice did not sound human. If they were words, Shane did not understand them. He stared into the ghost's eye and then looked past him again at Frank.

The other man was just getting to his knees, but the ghosts were close.

"Frank, move your ass!" Shane shouted.

The King growled and turned his head, still holding Shane in place. He leaned his head in and then roared once more. The sound was different, higher pitched.

The lurching, crawling ghosts reeled back as though they had been burned. They scuttled and clawed their way away from the King, Frank, and Shane, retreating to the shadows of the cabins or back under the snow.

With a second, shorter burst of a roar, the King returned his gaze to Shane. He dropped him to his feet and released his arms, pressing one hand into his throat and holding him firmly. His eye bore a hole into Shane's as he lifted his right hand, showing the damaged finger from before.

"GEEE SAHHH NITTT!" the King said again.

The pressure on Shane's neck was powerful. He could barely breathe, could not speak or even shake his head. He stared at the finger, unsure of what the ghost was saying.

A frustrated sound emerged from beneath the skull mask. The king growled, shook his head, and looked around. The other ghosts were still there, lurking in the shadows, but they feared him and whatever perceived threat his roar implied. They kept their distance for now.

Frank was on his feet again. His chin was covered in blood, and Shane watched as he came for the King, wielding the iron bar once more. And, once more, the King was aware he was coming.

The raging ghost pulled Shane away from the wall and spun him toward the other man. He held Shane like a shield in front of Frank. Another hissed word escaped his mouth, sounding like little more than a random noise to Shane.

"KAAAA-ILLLL," the ghost said.

Frank stood behind Shane, just off to the side. The iron rod was still in his hand. He could have taken a swing, and maybe made contact, but he seemed as curious now as Shane was about what the ghost was communicating.

"Kill?" Frank asked.

"KA-ILL," the King repeated.

"I don't... I don't understand. Kill what?" Frank asked.

It seemed risky to ask that question, but it had slowed the ghost. Shane did not understand what was happening, and it became less clear as the King's grip on his throat relaxed.

The spirit pulled his hand back and then balled it into a fist, beating his chest.

"KA-ILL," he said again. He showed his finger once more.

"KA-ILL."

"Kill... *you?*" Frank asked.

The King tilted his head, fixing his eye on Frank.

"KA-ILLY OO."

The words were garbled beneath the mask, gruff and inhuman. He was not used to speaking, and certainly not in English.

"You want me to kill you," Shane said.

The King fixed his gaze on Shane again. He knelt on the ground in front of him and reached behind his own back. Shane tensed as the ghost produced the bone blade that he had used earlier to attack him. He turned it swiftly in his hand, extending it toward Shane, handle first.

"Oh," Frank said softly.

The ghosts hiding in the shadows were making more noise now. Shane heard scattered moans, and some crept away from the buildings again. They were agitated, and the King seemed eminently aware of their reaction. He reached out, grabbed Shane's hands, and forced the bone blade into them. He held Shane's hand, the point of the blade directed at his scarred chest.

"Ka-ill," the King said softly.

There was a desperation in the way he spoke. The rage that was so profound in everything previously was replaced now by deep sadness and longing. Shane understood now what the ghost wanted. He wanted to die.

The island was not the same as the house on Berkley Street. When Vivienne was there working with the house, she was the malevolent force, and the house bent to her will. As powerful as the King was, the island was older. It had absorbed death and power and strength far more than the King ever had. The island did not work for the King; the King worked for the island.

When Shane had taken off the ghost's fingertip, he must have realized that he had found a way out. He had found someone who could destroy him, who could end whatever he had been enduring, however many centuries he had been stuck there as the barbaric tool of the island's will.

Shane stared into the wild eye hidden beneath the skull and realized it was much worse than that. The island didn't have a will. The King was not controlled by a thing that even thought. It was like being at the mercy of the tides, constantly bobbing in the waves. He could only move where it moved him. He could never rationalize with it, and he could never escape it. Until now.

"Okay." Shane nodded. He closed his fist around the cold handle of the bone knife. "Don't have to tell me again."

The King kept his hand in place and lowered his head, bending until the back of his skull was exposed.

Shane glanced at Frank, who was looking around the village at the bloated spirits that slowly crept closer.

"I don't think we have much time," Frank said.

"Don't need it," Shane replied.

He pulled his hand away from the King's in one swift, upward motion. He held the bone blade high and then swung down. The sharp tip pierced the back of the ghost's skull and drove deep.

Every part of Shane's body tensed. A sound escaped his lips that he couldn't account for. The force of the blast as the King's body came apart was like nothing else. The power was beyond anything he had imagined. It was like he had dropped a grenade in front of himself.

He collided with Frank, and both men were thrown backward against Alina's cabin, cracking one of the walls and half-collapsing the roof above their heads.

The village shook, and the assembled ghosts from the depths were launched backward as well. They scuttled away in the wake of the destruction, diving below again, desperate to free themselves, and leaving the village empty of all but Frank and Shane.

The island quaked. A tear appeared in the sky like a split in fabric, and Shane stared up at it from where he had landed, wincing in pain as his mouth filled with blood.

Light flashed through the night sky. The clouds parted, the night fell away, and it was no longer dark. It was midday, and the blue sky held a handful of clouds but little else.

Beneath them, the earth rumbled. The pulsing sound had returned, and the world shook in time with it.

The island was angry.

CHAPTER 26
BURN

Screams filled the air.

"Shane."

Frank's voice was strained. He sounded out of breath.

"Shane!"

"Yeah," Shane said.

The world shook. Alina's cabin collapsed, sending plumes of dust around them. Shane sat up, but his chest felt like it had been turned inside out. A few of his ribs had to be broken. Maybe more than a few.

He coughed, and there was blood in his mouth. He wasn't sure where it was coming from. The hole in his face was torn wider. He felt it with his tongue; the flesh of his cheek was ragged and open.

The screams were louder. Shane lifted his head and pain blossomed through his chest like a shockwave, radiating across his shoulders and back. He clenched his teeth and did his best to ignore it.

The dead had returned in droves. The half-rotten cave dwellers, the dried husks from the forest, and the mutilated villagers together this time. The island was sending everything it had. Real or illusory, it had summoned its full strength.

"They're everywhere," Frank said.

He was crouching at Shane's side, having taken less of the blast from the King's demise and coming out with only a bloody head wound to show.

"We need to go."

Shane chuckled and regretted it immediately when the pain felt like a brick being dropped on his lungs.

"Go where?"

"The Great Hall. The candlesticks are iron. And they can't sneak in unseen under the snow like out here," Frank suggested.

"Iron candlesticks," Shane said. "Sure."

Frank grabbed Shane by the arm and lifted him from the ground. Shane bit back a pained growl, and when Frank hesitated, he shook his head, using his own power to get to his feet. The effort took the wind out of him, but he ignored it. He didn't have time to worry about broken ribs or whatever else he might have suffered for destroying the King.

The dead swarmed like ants. Frank dug into his pocket with his free hand. He scattered another handful of iron shavings ahead of them and headed toward the Great Hall. Shane swung at anything that got close enough to grab at him, his iron ring making short work of ghosts trying to attack them.

"Last one." Frank tossed out another handful of iron across the narrow pathway that led to the Great Hall.

Every breath Shane took was painful, but he forced himself forward, matching Frank's pace and then exceeding it, making the other man move faster as well. They had an almost-clear path to the Great Hall door with only a few spirits blocking their path that were easily dispatched by an iron rod.

Shane pushed his way into the building while Frank stayed a step behind, swiping the iron rod through the heads of a pair of attacking spirits before joining him and closing the door. The interior of the Great Hall was cold and dark. The fires had been put out when everyone left, and aside from the two long tables, nothing was there.

"We can hold them off here and come up with a plan," Frank said. "We can take them one at a time if we have to."

Shane shook his head, leaning against one of the tables with an arm wrapped around his chest.

"There's no point," he said. "It's not the ghosts we need to fight; it's the island. It can only do so much. Maintaining all of this has to drain it somehow."

"Okay," Frank said. "How do we fight an island?"

The ghosts pushed their way in through the walls. Shane turned and looked back toward the kitchen. There were candlesticks on the tables, but there also were lanterns on the wall.

"They have fuel back there?"

Frank looked to the back as well and nodded.

He fought off the ghosts as they crept in while Shane labored toward the kitchen, grabbing a pair of thick, iron candlesticks as he went, swinging them like batons at anything that came close.

The kitchen was larger than he had anticipated, and he had no idea where anything was. He threw open cupboard doors until he found several canisters of kerosene.

"Frank," he shouted, drawing the other man to him.

"What are we burning?"

"Everything. We need to get to the woods."

They loaded as many of the canisters into Frank's bag as they could, and he secured it on his back, carrying one extra in his hand. When he was ready, they went back outside, with Frank taking point and Shane following. The ghosts were repopulating after Frank had banished so many with the iron filings, but Shane swung wide, not using any finesse and not needing to. The ghosts were still slow, clumsy, and only dangerous in numbers.

Each swing of his arms caused a jolt of pain through his chest, but he pressed on. They worked up the ridge toward the top of the bowl outside of the village, with Frank offering Shane a hand until they were on flat ground.

The snow covering the field was spotty, not particularly deep, and a welcome change from the last time Shane hiked across it. The progress was faster, and they reached the maple forest in minutes as a surge of crawling, limping, writhing spirits pursued them from the village.

Shane opened Frank's backpack when they reached the edge of the woods and pulled out a can of kerosene. With a wordless nod, the men split up, splashing the fuel across as many trees as they could. There was still dry ground cover throughout. The densely packed forest had remained free from much of the snow. It was a tinderbox waiting to go up.

They kept each other in sight and moved as quickly as they could. The ghosts were still slow but made progress, nonetheless. Shane wondered if the island understood what kerosene was. It must not have perceived a threat because it wasn't reacting as though it was in danger.

After emptying two more canisters, Shane and Frank arrived at the ring of stones in the center of the forest. Much of the woods would be untouched, but Shane hoped it would be enough. He bent and took a stick from the ground, pulling out his lighter, and setting it on fire. He wished he still had a cigarette, but he could wait until they were back on the mainland to pick up another pack.

"Let's go." He headed west as the first of the rotting ghosts crawled from the trees into the clearing.

The island could turn them around, sending them anywhere it wanted, but Shane hoped it would be too distracted to worry about them.

He threw the flaming stick toward the discarded canister of kerosene he'd left at the base of a cluster of maple trees. The fuel ignited quickly, climbing up the bark and trailing through the dry leaves on the forest floor. Fire raced in two directions, following his trail and the one Frank had laid. Tree after tree lit up, the fuel catching and then spreading to the bark and wood. Three trees became a dozen became a hundred.

The ground shook again, and the wind picked up. There were no clouds close enough to bring rain or snow, and as the wind blew, it spread the fire to more trees.

Some of the ghosts screamed, and the illusions of the villagers shouted threats and curses. Shane and Frank headed for the western edge of the island as the forest ignited, billowing black smoke into the air as the fire grew out of control.

The spread was faster than Shane expected, and it soon moved beyond the limits of where they had used the kerosene. The island's rage, and its confused attempt to make the problem go away, made it worse. The wind carried the fire to new trees and new sections of the woods.

Trees collapsed, with several falling into Shane and Frank's path. The fire moved ahead of them, outpacing them through the woods as the fierce wind spread it far and wide.

Some of the ghosts caught up as well, crawling from the earth among the flaming trees. They were easy enough to dispatch with the iron candlesticks Shane wielded, but it slowed their progress and allowed the fire to get farther ahead of them. They were forced to adjust their path several times to navigate around already-burning sections.

The sound of the fire soon drowned out everything else. Shane felt the heat at their backs. The crackling and snapping of wood was louder than the rumbling or the screams.

It wasn't until they reached the edge of the forest, with the western wall in sight, that Shane finally heard the ocean. They broke free of the forest, away from the spread of the flame, and Shane turned to look back. The sky was nearly black above the island, and the cloud of smoke was so large that it would likely be seen from both Maine and Nova Scotia. Probably even farther for anyone looking in that direction.

"There's the path." Frank pointed ahead.

Shane recognized the spot. The zigzagging stone path led down to the dock and from the top, he saw one boat tied up and waiting for them. His ribs hurt, and he still tasted blood in his mouth. The maple forest was engulfed now.

The fire roared louder than even the King. Wind whipped at it like it was pushing it toward them, but there was nothing to ignite between the forest and where the men stood. Smoke blew in their faces, and the heat washed over them, but all it did was melt the snow.

Some of the ghosts were still coming at them, but as the fire blazed, Shane watched more than one stop as though stunned, look around, and then dig itself back into the ground. It was as though they were waking up, freed from the island's influence for a moment. The damage was too much for the island to deal with. It could no longer maintain everything it was doing.

Frank led the way down the path toward the dock. Nothing came over the ridge after them. Even by the time they reached the wooden platform, there were no ghosts in pursuit. Shane waited until Frank was ready and had the engine started before throwing a leg over the edge of the boat, pulling the rope free, and watching the island fade behind them.

He looked up one last time at the ridge and there was something there, silhouetted by the glow of the raging fire. One figure, familiar but standing still and not pursuing. Hugh Carson lifted an arm to wave, and Shane returned the gesture. Frank saw him and looked over his shoulder as he piloted the boat out of the inlet.

"He survived," Frank said.

"Island's his now. Such as it is," Shane agreed.

"People will come when they see this," Frank pointed out. "That smoke is visible for miles."

"It should be fine for a while. That fire is everywhere. The island is going to need some time to recover. If it ever does."

"Yeah. Hope so," Frank replied.

In truth, that was a lot of hope on Shane's part as well. He didn't know for sure, but he knew it was weak.

It had to need time.

EPILOGUE

The gruff-looking man in the knit stocking cap nodded to Frank and walked away, heading down the dock toward whichever of the boats moored there was his. Frank sighed heavily, rubbing a hand on the back of his head, and looked at Shane.

"No one has seen Mo in days. Or his boat. Last place he said he was going was Maple Grove to look for us."

Shane lit a cigarette and nodded. It stung to breathe in the smoke, but he was still doing it. His ribs were wrapped, several were bruised, and some were broken. They had wanted him to go to a hospital, but he told the doctor at the clinic in town that he'd be fine.

No one would see Mo again, then. He seemed like a good man. He didn't deserve what happened to him. Another victim of the island, one no one even knew was taken until after it happened.

"He radioed in, said what he was up to, and then nothing. No debris from his boat, even."

"Place doesn't leave debris," Shane said. Nothing that might draw unwanted attention. Like a dog burying a bone, keeping it secret and keeping it safe.

There was not much to say about it. Shane felt for the man and for whatever family he'd left behind. He had been a man of his word, helping Shane and Frank, and living up to his end of the bargain they had struck. His ship had likely been dashed on the rocks, or some of the spirits guarding the place had killed him when he went ashore. Either way, it was nothing he deserved, and nothing he had bargained for. But there was also nothing to be done about it now.

How many years had that story repeated itself, Shane wondered. How many people ventured to the island, never to return? Thousands. It was an endlessly hungry thing that forever lured in more lives to consume. The King was just another victim. An exceptional one, but a victim, nonetheless. The island was insatiable.

There was nothing about the island burning in the local news. They had spent the night in a little motel just outside of town. The next morning, they expected it to be all anybody was talking about on the mainland. Surely, the smoke would have been visible from town. Surely, someone would have gone out in a boat to see the island scorched, a burning, raging inferno. Nothing of the sort happened. No one knew anything.

The fact that no one had noticed an island on fire would be perplexing under normal circumstances, but not with the island involved. Shane suggested they take one of the boats and go back to see.

They headed back together, barely speaking as Frank piloted the boat. The sky was mostly clear, and the sun was bright but pale. There was no smell in the air as they approached. Shane wasn't sure how the smell of a forest fire traveled over the open sea. He didn't know which direction the wind had taken the smoke, but the closer they got, he saw no remnants of what they had done.

There should have been wisps of smoke and ash from the smoldering woods, from the village, from something. Even after the island burned out, there should have been some sign. But when it came into view, when his eyes saw what lay ahead, he saw the treetops of the skeletal, winter-dead forest. He saw every tree, as alive as it had ever been.

"It's like it never happened," Frank said.

Shane thought that Frank might be righter than he thought. Anywhere else in the world, Shane would not have been so quick to say that. But on Maple Grove? The island was too powerful.

They might have burned it. That could have happened. But in Shane's mind, it was just as likely that the island refused to burn. It didn't allow the fire to take hold, it only showed it to them as they left. Maybe as a parting gift. Maybe a concession to convince them to stay away. He should have guessed, but leaving was the priority.

Frank reduced speed as they got closer to the island. Nothing about it looked any different from the day they'd first arrived, except the missing boats.

"Should we get closer?" Frank asked.

"Yeah," Shane said.

They headed in cautiously, and Frank piloted past the end of the dock, as close to the shore as they could. Shane went to the storage cupboard full of supplies, moving some rope and a rain jacket out of his way. A hatchet was in there, some cans of spray paint, and some other items.

"Come on." Shane got off the boat.

He set foot on the dock, not sure what he was expecting. Nothing happened. There was no shift in the weather, and no waterlogged hand from the depths grabbed at his ankle. It was unremarkable in every way.

Frank joined him, and the men left the dock and headed up the zigzagging path in the rocks. Shane had to see for himself what had happened. He didn't know why he needed to see it, but he still wanted to.

He saw Frank tense every time the breeze picked up along the face of the rocks. There was that fear that it was starting, that a storm would consume them, their boat would disappear, and they would be trapped again. It could have happened, but Shane's gut wasn't telling him that. Things were different without the King. Not totally, but different enough.

They reached the top, where the path first took them toward the village. Where they saw the forest for the first time, sprawling to the left with its aluminum buckets collecting sap.

There were no buckets now, and no path. What had once been barely there, just the result of years of foot traffic, was grown over. There was no snow on the island, just green grass, flaccid and depressed in the cold weather. The forest was untouched. No sign that people had ever been there. No sign that fire had ever raged.

The trees looked strong and healthy despite their lack of leaves. They were as densely packed as ever. Shane saw nothing among them. No moving shapes, and nothing watching them back.

"Should we check the village?" Frank asked.

"No," Shane said. "I don't think that's necessary."

They looked at one another for a moment, and Frank scratched the back of his neck.

"Do you feel that?" he asked.

Shane nodded. Something was there, something that was hard to explain. A feeling not unlike being watched, but something deeper than that. It was like someone standing right behind them that they couldn't see. And they were doing it on purpose. The island was very aware of them. And they were aware of it.

Frank turned, heading back down the path toward the dock. Shane spared one last look across the landscape. No ghosts, no Hugh, no anyone. Just the island. Just the raw power of the island radiating out of the ground. The power of thousands of dead over hundreds of years. Shane never wanted to see the place again.

Once they had reached the boat, Frank got on board and set about preparing to leave.

"Need a few minutes," Shane said, not joining him.

Shane took the hatchet and headed to the end of the dock. He dismantled it hastily, tearing apart the wooden planks and cutting them away from the support posts buried in the water. He worked quickly, not caring if his cuts were ugly or smooth. Chips shattered and flew as he tore away plank after plank.

He worked his way back, all the way down the dock, pulling out board after board, hacking at the support posts as best he could to remove the tops and leave the rest submerged.

He threw most of the wood into the water, but when he was close enough to shore, he threw several planks onto the land. By the time he reached Frank in the boat, there was nothing else to see in the water. The dock was gone, and there would be no invitation for people to come closer to land. Still, it was not enough.

Shane took the rope and headed to the tree on the shore that was closest to the water. He wedged several planks of wood against one of the branches, and then affixed more underneath, turning the planks into a large board, and using the rope to lash it together. It was not ideal, but it would hold up to the weather. Once he had it in place, he used the remainder of the rope to secure it tightly to the tree.

Frank said nothing as he watched Shane work. He stood on the deck of the boat, leaning against the gunwale with his arms crossed.

Shane took the spray paint and pondered what to write for a moment. He did not have a lot of space, and he needed it to be seen from the water if anyone approached. Eventually, he settled on a simple, short message. "NO TRESPASSING" in big, block letters.

The island was good about keeping people away. The very nature of a haunted place caused a feeling that most people didn't like. It normally kept people like Mo away. But it also attracted those who felt the lure of the mysterious. Maybe the island targeted them. Shane thought some would still likely approach, but some would be dissuaded when they saw no dock and a sign warning them to leave. It might save a life or two. He could do little else.

When the sign was as secure as Shane could make it, he returned to the boat. Frank started the engine, and they pulled away slowly. It took some time and caution to navigate through the rocks and hidden hazards in the water. It was unsafe to speed out of the inlet and away from Maple Grove.

As they drifted away, Shane watched a figure near the top of the path drift out of view. It had only been there for an instant, barely more than a shadow. The sort of thing you aren't sure you even saw from the corner of your eye. But Shane was sure.

"Clear of the rocks." Frank accelerated into the open sea. "You see something?"

"Nothing unusual," Shane said. He almost pitied whoever landed on Maple Grove next. But someone would, sooner or later.

He lit another cigarette and exhaled a puff of smoke. The sky was clear now, and the weather had become warmer. The sea was calm, and the sun was bright. The island looked inviting. It looked like a mystery waiting to be discovered.

Sooner or later, he thought. *It will get to feed again.*

— ⬥ —

Check out these best-selling series from our talented authors:

GHOST STORIES

RON RIPLEY

BERKLEY STREET SERIES
MOVING IN SERIES
HAUNTED COLLECTION SERIES
DEATH HUNTER SERIES

IAN FORTEY

JIGSAW OF SOULS SERIES
CULT OF THE ENDLESS NIGHT SERIES

SUPERNATURAL SUSPENSE

A. I. NASSER

SLAUGHTER SERIES
SIN SERIES

DAVID LONGHORN

NIGHTMARE SERIES
ASYLUM SERIES

SARA CLANCY

THE BELL WITCH SERIES
BANSHEE SERIES

For a complete list of our new releases and best-selling horror books, visit
ScareStreet.com or scan the QR code below!